STAR WARS™

STORIES OF
JEDI AND SITH

WRITTEN BY

ROSEANNE A. BROWN • SARWAT CHADDA

DELILAH S. DAWSON • TESSA GRATTON

MICHAEL KOGGE • SAM MAGGS • MICHAEL MORECI

ALEX SEGURA • VERA STRANGE • KAREN STRONG

EDITED BY

JENNIFER HEDDLE

Disney • LUCASFILM PRESS

Los Angeles • New York

For information address Disney • Lucasfilm Press,
1200 Grand Central Avenue, Glendale, California 91201.

Printed in the United States of America

First Edition, June 2022

1 3 5 7 9 10 8 6 4 2

FAC-034274-22112

ISBN 978-1-368-08054-5

Library of Congress Control Number on file

Visit the official *Star Wars* website at: www.starwars.com.

CONTENTS

INTRODUCTION

WHAT DOES IT MEAN TO BE GOOD? It's one of life's eternal questions, with many possible answers, and not one that can be resolved in this short introduction! But when I think about the *effort* to be a good person, the Jedi come to mind as an example of those who always at least try to be good. None of us are perfect, including the Jedi, but Jedi Knights give us an ideal to strive for. Whether it's Luke standing tall and refusing to strike down his father, or Obi-Wan taking on a young Padawan because he thinks it's the right thing to do, or Rey fighting against the evil of Palpatine, *Star Wars* provides us with plenty of heroes on the side of the light, doing everything they can to push back the darkness.

But of course you can't have that light *without* the darkness, or good without evil. And *Star Wars* has no shortage of memorable villains, too. From the demonic-looking Darth Maul to the twisted and vile Palpatine to the undeniably iconic Dark Lord of the Sith himself, Darth Vader, evil is always there for the Jedi to face in their fight for the light. (Then there are those like Asajj Ventress who live in the shadows between, reminding us that the definitions of "good" and "bad" are not always black-and-white!)

I'm so pleased to present ten exciting original stories by a group of incredible authors, stories that explore what it is to be good, bad, and everything in between. There are some important questions asked here—What makes a Jedi? What does it mean to stand for justice? In a complicated galaxy, what's really the right thing to do?—but there's also thrilling action, adventure, and humor, in timeless *Star Wars* stories that feel like they've jumped straight off a movie screen. So enjoy—and choose your side!

—Jennifer Heddle

A long time ago in a galaxy far,
far away. . . .

WHAT A JEDI MAKES

MICHAEL KOGGE

THE TEMPLE LOOMED AHEAD, pink in the dawn, just as it had in the boy's dreams.

It was a massive structure of stone, with a trapezoidal body on a rectangular base. Five towers crowned its flat top, four on each corner, with the fifth and tallest rising from the center. According to legend it had been erected on the summit of a mountain when mountains still dominated the planet's terrain. After millennia of expansion, the Temple itself was the only mountain in this district of the city, drawing the eye from every direction.

Yet what lay within could not be glimpsed from without. Few viewports penetrated the Temple's sloped sides. The stained-glass windows along its front arcade permitted only light to pass, not curious glances. Occasionally a robed figure could be observed on a tower balcony, but these silhouettes revealed little.

This was not to say the residents of the Temple were reclusive. They were in fact some of the most recognizable individuals in the Republic, members of a mystical fellowship of warriors, healers, diplomats, and thinkers graced with extraordinary powers of mind and muscle. Rather than using their gifts for selfish gain, they had pledged their lives to defend peace and justice in an ever-perilous galaxy. Yet how they attained their astonishing abilities remained mostly a mystery. Out of the trillions of beings in the galaxy, only a select few were permitted to master the secrets taught inside the Temple.

The boy would soon join that small number. He would gain admittance to the Temple and learn the truth about what was called the Force. He would become that which he had always dreamed of being.

A Jedi.

As he approached the Temple, the boy stuck to the shadows wherever he could, skirting down alleys and skipping across roofs, avoiding skybridges and crawling along pipelines. Someone like him was unwelcome on the upper levels of Coruscant. Unlike the wealthy who lived on the city planet's surface and could afford the best in fashion, he was dressed in rags and smelled of sewage. His feet were bare and dirty, and his hair was patchy, cut by a rough blade. Filth was indistinguishable from the freckles on his face, and what flesh of his that could be seen under the grime was pale, rarely exposed to the sun. Though he was biologically human, few of his fellow species would regard him as such. He was of a class of beings that society shunned.

The boy was an orphan from the undercity.

Supreme Chancellor Lina Soh liked to say, "We are all the Republic," but in reality there were many who remained on society's fringes despite Soh's best efforts to eliminate old prejudices. Rich surface dwellers on Coruscant still feared outcasts like the boy would infect their districts with disease, poverty, and crime. If he was caught wandering about, he'd be branded a pickpocket and sent back down into the slums. No one would shed a tear at his disappearance.

His lowborn background would not matter to the Jedi, however. In all the datafiles he'd read, the newsvids he'd watched, the stories he'd heard, the Jedi respected beings from all walks of life. The diversity of their ranks reflected this openness. Some of the greatest Knights had been nobles, others nobodies. A few had once been enslaved. A street kid like him would be in good company.

The boy bolted past a block of government buildings and arrived at Processional Way, the main boulevard that led to the Temple. There was nowhere to hide, no shadows or nooks, but he was not worried. Usually the avenue was flooded with all manner of people—Jedi, bureaucrats, activists, and tourists—but at this early hour, not even the trinket peddlers had arrived to set up their stalls. The boy was alone, and happily so, holding his head high as he strode toward the Temple. Destiny and destination were one and the same, so said the old Masters.

"Halt!"

A girl in sand-colored robes dashed toward him. She appeared to be an indeterminate mix of species, with both skull spines and head-tails poking out from shoulder-length nut-brown hair. Her gold eyes dazzled and her emerald skin glinted in the morning light. She was both beautiful and fierce, and he stopped at her command.

"Drop your weapons, Ganzee goon, and don't move," she said, igniting a blue-bladed lightsaber.

The boy opened his hands. "I don't have any weapons. And I'm not Ganzee, I swear." The Ganzee were a notorious criminal gang from the undercity who recruited orphans like him to do their dirty work. He had eluded all their attempts to lure him, going so far as to hide in the gutters whenever he spotted them.

"But you look like Ganzee, smell like Ganzee,

too." The girl's face puckered and she fanned the air. "Stars save me, do you bathe with banthas?"

The boy wanted to remark that her scent of cleansing chemicals smelled equally unpleasant, but he kept that to himself. "I've never seen a bantha, actually. I'm from level thirteen-twelve of the undercity. I've come to train as a Jedi."

She seemed perplexed. "There was no mention of a new arrival. Which Master sent for you?"

"I came by myself."

She snorted. "This must be some kind of prank. Something Master Elzar put you up to. To fool me, get me off my game. Because no one just walks up to the Temple and demands to be trained."

"I'm not here to fool anyone or demand anything," the boy said. "Coming here's more like . . . a dream I've always had. I've even brought documentation to show I make a good candidate."

"Documentation?"

"Blood tests. They have my midi-chlorian count."
The boy pulled out a flimsi from his rags. During his
research, he'd discovered that the Jedi often examined a candidate's blood for microscopic organisms
they called midi-chlorians. The greater the number,
the stronger a candidate's suitability to join the Order.
Anticipating the Jedi would request a count, the boy
had paid an Ortolan bloodletter to perform a test. He
proudly pointed out the results to the girl. "As you can
see, my count is high."

The girl only glanced at it. "No Master with any
common sense cares about blood tests. When they
search for younglings, they need proof of talent,
not . . . paperwork."

Her criticism didn't worry him. He was ready for
such a request. "Of course," he said. "How's this?"

Pocketing the flimsi, he inhaled, then did what
he'd practiced so long in the sewers. He jumped up
as high as he could, folded his knees to his chest, and

executed a somersault in midair like he saw Jedi do in holovids. Coming down, he botched the landing with a misstep but quickly recovered and smiled.

The girl shrugged. "Any acrobat could do that. What the Masters seek is an ability to do things that ordinary beings cannot. And anyways, they'll say you're too old."

"Too old? How old are you?"

"Fourteen standard years."

"Same as me," the boy said. "Why should that make a difference?"

"Because I was brought to the Temple when I was an infant. You're too old to start training."

Her attitude was beginning to annoy him. "Can't you talk to the Masters for me? I can show them I'm ready."

"It's not my place to do that. I'm only an Initiate. A Master hasn't even chosen me as a Padawan yet."

"So let me do it," the boy said. "Who do I talk to?"

The girl deactivated her blade. "Look, I'm investigating a dire threat and should alert security if I find anyone suspicious. You seem like a nice kid, so I won't. But I advise you leave before the police and Temple Guards make their sweep." She checked her wrist chrono. "Which should be any moment now. Good luck."

The girl offered a brief—and to him, false—smile and then spun away. With a few running leaps, she was off.

The boy stood alone in a state of shock. He'd expected tough questions, even an entrance exam, but never a flat-out refusal, especially from someone his own age. This was most definitely never a part of his dreams.

Then he heard a strange melody being hummed at the edge of the boulevard, where rows of flowers bloomed. The boy walked over to see.

A small figure dressed in the Jedi's gold-and-white

Temple robes was watering the plants. A gnarled hand held a curved walking stick, and long pointy ears protruded from a round head that was wisped with white hair. The boy could identify all the members of the Jedi Council, and there was only one Jedi this could be.

"Master Yoda?"

The figure stopped humming and shifted toward the boy. Yes, it had to be him. No Jedi was so wrinkled with age. Or so small and green. Or had such tiny sharp teeth, which he showed in a mischievous grin.

The boy stepped forward. "Master Yoda, I—"

In the sky above screamed a triple-finned airspeeder, with lights strobing atop the cockpit. A voice boomed from an external comm. "This is the Temple District Police. We are looking for suspects in a criminal matter. Remain there for questioning. A holding ray will be deployed if necessary."

The boy did not doubt what would happen to him

if he obeyed. The police would never believe that he came to train. They'd say he came to steal.

He turned and ran.

His acrobatics proved lifesaving. He ducked and dodged the ray aimed at him. It captured flowers instead, causing Yoda to shake his fist at the sky.

The boy fled into the city. He was safe, but his dream was in danger. Now he was wanted.

Hours later, the boy huddled behind an upscale eatery. The smart thing to do would be to get far away from this district. The police knew what he looked like and would be searching for him. If they nabbed him, his punishment would be far more severe than a one-way ticket back to the lower levels.

But he wasn't leaving. Not after what had happened at the Temple. One of the greatest Jedi of this age had smiled—at him. An orphan from the under-city. A nobody.

This acknowledgment could mean nothing, of course. But he was going to find out. He would try again.

This time he would dress the part.

He crouched under a water spigot and washed off as much grime as he could. Then he gathered clothing for his new outfit. He grabbed trousers from the basket of a laundry droid. Pulled a tunic from a charity bin. Fashioned a utility belt from a discarded loop of comm cable. Swiped a pair of black boots from the front door of a luxury apartment, stuffing the toes with crumpled napkins to ensure a proper fit. For the most visible article of his wardrobe, he snuck into a costume shop and took a brown robe intended for masquerade balls.

He dressed himself in his new clothes, leaving on his rags as undergarments. A check of his reflection in an airspeeder window showed that he was close to looking convincing.

He was just missing one major detail.

At a construction site, he collected a set of tools that included a plasma torch. He braved a public refresher and unscrewed the drainpipe from the sink. In a scrap yard, he yanked an activation button from a YT-series dashboard and a lens dish from a sensor array. Last but not least, he snagged magnetic couplers from the chargers at a refueling station.

Having retrieved what he needed, he retired to a dark corner of a speeder garage. Within a few hours, he manufactured something out of the parts that resembled a Jedi lightsaber.

It was far from the real thing and should never be used as an actual weapon. The blue plasma beam that blazed from the drainpipe was erratic, unable to hold together for long before fizzling out. But a few seconds of stability was better than none, and the beam's low power meant he wouldn't accidentally chop off his own arm if he mishandled the device.

After a bit of tinkering with the magnetic couplers, he hung the lightsaber hilt off his belt, adjusted his robes, and departed the speeder garage. Now for the final test.

He went out into the midday streets. At first he stayed clear of any crowds. But when no one gave him a second glance, he grew confident that his disguise was working and walked more freely among the pedestrians.

Then came the police cruiser.

It was the same triple-fin that had harassed him at the Temple. Swerving in traffic, it dropped from the skylanes to hover beside him. A pane on its canopy opened.

"Hey, Padawan," chirped the pilot inside, an orange-scaled Kadrillian in a police uniform that accommodated his terrapin half shell. "Looking for a human youngling 'bout your age, dirty under-dweller type. Think he's related to the Ganzee Gang. Word is they're about to try something. Don't know what. Seen anyone like that sneaking around?"

The boy shook his head, scanning for the nearest

alley to book down if necessary. There was nothing within fifty meters.

"Well, let me know if you do." The officer leaned his head out of the window. "Say, I don't think we've met before. I'm Detective Tals Trilby, Temple District Police. What's your name?"

It was a question the boy hadn't been asked in years. Fortunately, chatter on the officer's comm saved him from having to respond.

"Shoot—can't chat, gotta run. Some theft at Three-Yees Costume Shop," Trilby said. "But keep an eye out for anything suspicious. 'Cause my wise old breakfast pal says you Jedi younglings see things others don't." The pane closed, and the airspeeder zoomed away.

The boy sighed in relief. He also felt something he'd rarely felt before.

Respect.

So that was what it was to be a Jedi. The cops came to *you* for help.

For the rest of the afternoon, he roamed the city blocks around the Temple, waiting for the right opportunity to return.

It occurred when a group of Jedi younglings, some years his junior, were led past by an older chaperone. Among the younglings were humans, snaggle-toothed Snivvians, star-shaped Conjeni, respirator-wearing Gand, and trunk-nosed Kubaz. Most wore Jedi robes, though a handful were dripping wet in swimsuits, their clothes folded under their arms. They must have had an outing at a local pool. The day was a scorcher. Heat rose from the pavement and hoods were worn as shade.

The boy followed the group, pulling his own hood up. The younglings were so rambunctious and the chaperone so busy wrangling them that no one noticed him tagging along. It was just as well, because the chaperone was the girl who had stopped him at dawn.

As they neared the Temple, the boy sensed others were trailing the group. His awareness was nothing like what the Jedi possessed, but rather an instinct he'd developed to survive in the undercity. Glances over his shoulder, however, revealed only pedestrians hurrying through the day's shimmering heat. No one appeared suspicious.

Still, the feeling did not leave him.

Once the group came to Processional Way, the girl snapped her fingers and the younglings quieted and fell into a straight line. The boy brought up the rear.

The boulevard ended in a triple staircase of polished marble, topped by four giant statues of the Temple's founders. The group ascended the center staircase, and the boy got his first view of the Temple entrance. In place of gates, there were three rows of four stone pylons, the front featuring carvings of the Four Founders. Between the monoliths stood three masked sentinels armed with the cylindrical hilts of double-bladed lightsaber pikes. These were the Temple Guards, an elite corps of Jedi chosen to defend the Temple against intruders. So exceptional were they in combat that it was rumored in ages past a mere three had turned back an army of three thousand. They were not to be trifled with.

The center guard moved to allow two Jedi to emerge from the Temple. One was a human woman in a white tunic and cape with a circlet around her blond hair. The boy recognized her as Avar Kriss, a well-known Jedi Master. Her companion was much shorter—and greener. "Greetings, Clan Kowak," Master Yoda said, leaning on his walking stick. "Swimming lesson went well?"

The Kubaz younglings issued gleeful snorts. The Gand exhaled gas from their respirators. And the humans, Conjeni, and Snivvians shouted back, among many things, "Amazing," "Wizard," and "Can we go back tomorrow?"

Yoda chuckled. "Good to exercise the body, time now to exercise the mind. Meditate we will and swim through the currents of the Force. Come. Master Kriss is back from an important mission and will teach you this afternoon." He gestured to Kriss, who smiled, and then they both walked back through the pylons. The younglings followed them while the boy, as last in line, crested the final steps.

He had that feeling again.

He looked behind him, down the stairs, across Processional Way. The boulevard was vacant but for the ghostly glint of heat rising from the road.

What was odd was that the heat waves had discernable forms. The contours seemed to resemble two humanoid bodies. And they were moving toward the stairs.

Someone grabbed the boy from behind and pushed him against the base of a statue. "You're not part of this class," said the girl.

"Let me go." He wiggled free of her grip, but the hood fell from his face. The girl's eyes widened when she saw who he was. "You again?"

"I'm here to tell you your group was being followed," he said.

"What? Where? By whom?"

The boy pointed down the steps. "See the shimmer, the waves of heat?"

The girl stared in that direction. "I see nothing."

The boy craned his neck to look. He could see clear across Processional Way. The girl was right. There was nothing strange out there. No shimmer of heat at all. "But they were just there. I saw them. Following."

"The only follower is you." The girl tugged on his robes. "Dressed like a Jedi, obviously trying to sneak your way into the Temple."

"Let me speak to a Master. I can explain."

"Didn't you hear me before? That's not how it works. Even if you were of age, you'd need proof of your talent to be considered, not a costume." She indicated the lightsaber hanging from his belt. "Where'd you steal that from?"

"I built it."

"Nonsense."

He unclipped it from his belt and offered it to her. "Try it."

Unlike the flimsi, she took it and turned it from side to side, then thumbed the activator. A bluish beam erupted from the lens on the hilt and kept its form as she swung it. "You built this? Impressive."

The boy smiled at the compliment. "Thanks."

She made one huge arc, then switched off the blade. "But not a lightsaber. A lightsaber has a presence in the Force. This is nothing more than a tightly focused welding torch."

The boy grew angry. Who did she think she was? She wasn't even a full Padawan yet, let alone a Jedi. "You're wrong. The Force is strong with this blade," he said, reaching out a hand, "as it is with me."

The lightsaber sprang from her grasp into his. "That enough proof for you?"

She narrowed her eyes at him, as if she was trying to look through him, or around him, or inside him. Whatever she was doing, it unnerved him. "Stop that," he said.

"Then stop pretending to be someone you're not."

She blinked, broke her stare. "Because if you were what you say you are, a Master would have already found you."

The boy was not going to let this one girl—this *Initiate*—determine his fate. "Well, they didn't find me. They missed me. That's why I've come to them."

The girl raised her hands. "Fine. Go to the Temple Guards. Let them be the judge. Maybe they won't see you as a kid playing Jedi."

At the entrance, the three silent sentinels gripped their lightsaber pikes. The middle guard had returned to block the path Yoda and the younglings had taken into the Temple. All seemed to look in the boy's direction. No doubt if he went to them, they'd alert the police.

The boy gritted his teeth. He wouldn't get anywhere this time. He'd have to come back when this girl wasn't around.

He turned and walked down the stairs.

"May the Force be with you," she said in parting.

He didn't let her see the pain on his face. Her words cut deep.

In the dark corner of the speeder garage, the boy sat with his legs crossed. His makeshift lightsaber lay an arm's length away. He had switched off the magnetic coupler under his sleeve, requiring him to rely on himself to move the saber, not some technical trick.

The boy closed his eyes, relaxed his body, and like he had on so many other occasions, stretched out his hand. "The Jedi and the lightsaber," he said, reciting a mantra he'd decoded from an old datatape he'd located, "the lightsaber and the Jedi. The two are one. The Force . . . the Force binds us."

He imagined the lightsaber starting to rattle, then rolling from side to side. "The Force calls my lightsaber," he continued, flexing his fingers, "the Force calls my lightsaber . . . to me."

In his mind he saw the lightsaber slide along the

duracrete and rise into the air to land softly in his palm. His hand tingled. His fingers twitched. At last, he had finally done it.

When he opened his eyes, the lightsaber lay on the ground where he had placed it, in the same position, unmoved. It was just like every other time he'd tried. A failure. An impossibility.

He bowed his head. He'd known it would eventually come to this, that he'd have to demonstrate his ability in the Force to be a Jedi. Yet he had purposefully ignored his own fundamental flaw. For how could he ever be accepted into the Jedi Order when he could not do what all Jedi could? He had lied when he told the girl he was strong in the Force.

He could not feel the Force at all.

The boy sat in the dark corner, alone with his thoughts, until it was dark outside. He had followed his dream, and it had led him here, to the surface, yet still—always—in the dark.

He left the garage in the dead of night. The few beings on the streets avoided him just as he avoided them. Unfortunately, he couldn't avoid Processional Way. The route toward the district center took him along the edge of the boulevard, where the flowers grew. The mountainous Temple loomed over him, glowing in the night, illuminated by ground fixtures and signal lights. It looked nothing like in his dreams.

He turned his back on the Temple and proceeded toward the district hub, where he could order a turbolift down to the lower levels. It was time to surrender his childhood fantasies. It was time to accept who he was and go back where he belonged.

Then he had that feeling again. Someone or something was behind him.

He peered over his shoulder. A cloud shimmered on the boulevard and was moving away from the Temple.

This couldn't be a phenomenon of heat. The temperature had cooled considerably since the afternoon.

"Help," cried a voice in the cloud.

The boy had heard similar pleas on a daily basis where he was from. It was pointless to do anything about them, as much as he'd wanted to. In the under-city, survival depended on staying clear of everyone's business. Those who helped got hurt.

He took a few more steps when the cry was repeated, more insistent. He glimpsed strange spectral shapes in the shimmering air. Outlines of a head, arm, legs. The cloud shifted back and forth, as if trying to keep something—or someone—inside of it.

He kept walking. This was a problem for the surface dwellers, not a poor orphan.

A third cry, even louder. "Help!"

The boy halted. He took one last look. The shimmering cloud floated near the end of the boulevard. Soon it would be out of the Temple's light and disappear into the shadows. If he wanted to do something, this would be his only chance. And if he didn't do something, he knew he'd hear those cries the rest of his life.

He unclipped the lightsaber from his belt and faced the cloud. "Stop," he said.

The cloud rolled toward him.

He pressed the activator on the drainpipe, igniting the blue beam. It might not have the strength to cut bone, but it could be useful in other ways.

He threw the saber at the cloud.

The beam crackled against shimmering waves as if it had hit an invisible wall, then fizzled out as the hilt fell to the ground. But the cloud began to ripple and resolve, revealing three solid humanoid forms. Two were clad head to toe in black bodysuits that sparked with electricity. Parts of their bodies flashed invisible, then visible, until they stayed that way.

The boy's gamble had paid off. His attack had disrupted the suits' circuitry.

The third figure must have been concealed in an

overlapping field, for she wore no such suit. Dressed in torn Jedi robes, she was none other than the girl from the Temple.

Her captors held her by the arms. She kicked but was too weak to free herself. Seeing the boy, she tried to speak, but a captor smacked her in the face. Her eyes fluttered and head drooped.

Her captors let go of her to draw their holstered blasters.

The boy triggered the magnetic coupler in his sleeve and waved his hand. The lightsaber whipped up from the ground into his grasp. Then he executed the jump he had practiced for so long in the sewers, adding one very Jedi-like move.

As he somersaulted in midair, eluding their stun bolts, he activated his lightsaber again and swung. The plasma welding beam held together long enough to strike both pistols. The blasters smoked, and the two kidnappers dropped them.

The boy landed on both feet, without stumbling,

as a Jedi would. "Don't make this situation worse," he said to the intruders.

They drew knives from hidden sheaths and leapt at the boy. He fell to his knees, losing his lightsaber, which rolled behind the attackers. Blade points poked his neck. What he'd feared in the undercity seemed true on the surface. Those who helped got hurt.

Yet he wasn't afraid. A calm came over him as he stared up at the hoods that covered his assailants' faces. If these were the last breaths he took, he would have no regrets. He had come to the surface, and even if he had not entered the Temple, he had lived out his dream.

The blade tips never made more than dots on his neck. There was a crack, another crack, and both adversaries tumbled to the ground, their heads bashed from behind.

The girl stood over them, holding the boy's lightsaber. "A drainpipe. Ingenious for a hilt. Makes a great club." She tossed the device to the boy.

He caught it and got to his feet. "I thought you were down and out."

She gingerly touched her cheek and winced. "I thought I was, too."

"Well, I was a goner. Thank you."

"You deserve all the thanks, not me. I'd be in a terrible place if you hadn't intervened." She bent down to one of her unconscious captors and retrieved her lightsaber from a pouch.

"These are the Ganzee gang members you were after?" the boy asked.

The girl nodded. "Even more than that."

Before he could inquire further, a bright light shone down on them. "This is the Temple District Police," a voice boomed from an approaching tri-finned speeder. "Remain where you are for questioning."

The girl checked her chrono. "A few minutes ahead of schedule today. How's that for timing?"

The speeder parked near them, and its canopy swished open. "Don't move, anyone," Detective

Trilby said. He heaved his bulk out of the pilot's seat. But his diminutive passenger beat him to the ground first, hopping out and ambling over to the younglings.

"All this pandemonium, and so early," Master Yoda said. He seemed smaller in person, yet more imposing.

The boy froze, and the girl straightened. "Ganzee kidnappers," she said. "We stopped them."

"That I see," Master Yoda said, examining the bodies.

Trilby plodded up for a look himself. "They wearing some kind of tech?"

"It made them invisible," the girl said.

"Shadowsuits? Thought those were still experimental," the detective said. "But if they do work, how'd you ever see these thugs?"

"I didn't. He did." The girl motioned to the boy.

Noticing the boy, Trilby gave him a big smile. "Ah! My friend from yesterday! Tell me your secret."

"I saw a shimmer," said the boy.

"A shimmer?"

"That's really all I saw."

"Okay, have to remember that. 'Cause someone'll try to use this tech again," Trilby said. "Teenine-Beenine, get these worms locked up before they start wriggling."

A silver detention droid detached from the speeder's underside and hovered over to the bodies. Pincer arms grabbed them and dragged them into a hold in the speeder's rear.

Trilby patted the boy's shoulder with a scaly hand. "A job well done, kid. You young Jedi have a keen eye, that's for sure."

Yoda arched an eyebrow at the boy. The boy knew he couldn't misrepresent himself in front of a Master of Yoda's stature. "Actually, I'm . . . I'm not a Jedi."

Trilby peered down at him. "Not a Jedi?"

"No."

"But you have a lightsaber. You're wearing the robes."

"The lightsaber's a fake. And these robes . . . they're not mine."

Trilby's eyes bulged. "You're the thief who stole from the costume shop!"

The boy ground his teeth. "But I plan to return everything."

"That's not how it goes, kid. I should book you for robbery and impersonating a Jedi. Teenine—"

The girl blocked the droid's path. "The boy's not a thief. He was assisting my investigation and needed a disguise. So he borrowed what he had to—which a Jedi can legally do in emergencies."

"But he just said he's not a Jedi," Trilby said.

The girl addressed Yoda. "Maybe he should be."

The boy could hardly believe what he'd just heard. After all her denials, she was advocating for him.

Yoda rested his hands atop his walking stick. He looked up at the boy. "A Jedi, eh?"

"It's all I've ever wanted to be, Master," the boy said. "It's why I came to the Temple. But—" He hesitated. He'd dreamed of this moment, when he would explain why he deserved to join the Order. Yet he could think only of the reasons why he didn't. "I know I'm too old—"

"Too old for what? To learn?" Yoda asked. "Over six hundred years of age am I, and still a student."

"Yes, but . . . my blood test. It's not right."

Yoda's brow creased with more wrinkles. "Your blood test?"

The girl chimed in. "He showed me his midi-chlorian count, Master."

"A count that's false," the boy said. "I paid for the results I wanted. I honestly couldn't tell you what my real count is."

"Midi-chlorians?" Yoda snickered. "You think midi-chlorians are what make a Jedi?"

"No, the Force is what makes a Jedi." The boy lowered his head. "And that's the one thing I don't have."

Yoda stopped laughing. "What do you mean you don't have the Force?"

"I can't call on it. Not like you. Not like her. I can't summon a lightsaber to my hand without trickery. I can't read people's minds. I can't feel it—the Force—at all. I'm just . . . ordinary." The boy turned away in shame.

Yoda huffed. "Then never a Jedi you will be, if that is what you believe." He started toward the speeder. "Detective, hungry are you for our morning porridge?"

"Always." Trilby rubbed his stomach. "Kid, if you don't return those clothes by midday, I'm tossing you in the slammer. Got it?"

The boy ignored the detective, as his mind was trying to decipher what Yoda's riddle had implied. It could only be—

He ran to catch up with the Jedi Master. "Wait—you mean, I *can* be a Jedi?"

Yoda stopped and scowled. "Study you should, the Farseeker Lyr. No great power had he, yet from his ink sprang some of the Jedi's greatest texts. For though the Jedi and the Force are one, the Force is not what a Jedi makes."

The boy frowned. "Then what makes a Jedi?"

Yoda jabbed him in the chest with his cane. "That is something only you can answer."

"I will," the boy said after a moment. "I want to be a Jedi—I believe I can be a Jedi."

"Have you a teacher?"

The boy looked at Yoda, who in turn looked at the girl out of the corner of his eye. "Oh, no," she said, backpedaling. "I'm only an Initiate."

"But you found me," the boy said.

Yoda nodded. "Found him you did. Teach him you shall. The way of the Jedi that is."

The girl trembled, pulling at her fingers, obviously flustered by what Yoda had proposed. "But what will he be? He's too old to train to be a Knight."

"More than Knights the Jedi Order is. Watchers, stewards, caregivers also, of these flowers, the grounds, our home," Yoda said, gesturing with his stick. He regarded the boy once more. "A guardian of the Temple you can be, if ready are you."

"Yes, yes, Master, I am ready."

"Regarding that, my friend . . ." Yoda flashed his mischievous grin. "We will see. We will see."

The little Jedi hopped into the speeder, then he and the detective were gone and the boy and girl were alone. It was strangely uncomfortable.

The boy finally broke the silence, divulging something he hadn't told anyone in years. "My name's Lohim . . . Lohim Nara."

The girl looked at him, and this time there was no judgment in her eyes. Just the same nervousness he felt. "I'm Reina Bilass," she said, "or that's my chosen name. My childhood name was Reina Ganzee."

The boy blinked, not expecting this. "As in—"

"The Ganzee are family," she said. "They brought me to the Temple when they realized I was different than the rest. Now they're threatening my clan, but it's me they really want back."

"To use your Jedi talent for their crimes," the boy added.

"I guess so."

They both watched the police speeder fade into the morning traffic. "I'll be honest. I never thought you of all people would be from the undercity," the boy said.

"Born on level eleven-eighty, supposedly," she said. "Kidnapped and then raised by the Ganzee on level ten-fourteen for a year, though of course I don't remember that."

"Better you don't. That's a rough level."

"So I've heard," the girl said.

The boy shook his head in disbelief. This girl— Reina—was like him. An orphan.

"I've got a lot to learn," he said.

"We both do," she said.

They walked up Processional Way together. The Temple loomed ahead, pink in the dawn, just as it had in the boy's dreams.

RESOLVE

ALEX SEGURA

QUI-GON JINN WAS ON EDGE long before his boots touched Desinta's ice-crusted ground.

He had been summoned hastily to the Outer Rim planet, and ushered to the surface under cloak and shadow. No one was to know he was there; no one was to know a Jedi had landed.

It was very much unlike the Jedi Council to practice such—if not outright deceit, then camouflage, Qui-Gon thought. He was greeted by a dozen or so Desintian guards. Part show of respect, part show of alarm. The planet's government was barely holding on to its rule, the world rife with crime and rotating revolutionaries. If Qui-Gon was being honest with himself, which he often was, this planet didn't matter much in the grand scope of the galaxy, or in the Jedi's efforts to secure the Republic. But it mattered enough.

"We need you to handle this the right way," Mace Windu had said to Qui-Gon on Coruscant on the eve of his departure. "Don't overthink it. Don't wonder what it means. Just get her back."

Just get her back.

The words hung over Qui-Gon as he scanned the massive docking bay, which had certainly seen better days. Droids skittered about, hastily repairing the few ships that remained. Workers yelled orders across the cavernous space. This was a planet at war with itself, and you could see the effects in every aspect of life.

But Mace Windu's words didn't refer just to this mission, this moment. It was a larger comment, Qui-Gon knew. It was as much about Qui-Gon and the decision that was looming over him as anything else. He couldn't help wondering, was this a test? A challenge that would answer the Council's request more clearly than anything Qui-Gon could say himself?

Before Qui-Gon could put more thought into the discussion, the soldiers stationed in front of him parted, creating a wide path. He heard the footsteps before he saw the lithe form of Prefect Aminar, the nominally elected leader of the planet. She was followed by two regents on either side, both wearing long green cloaks that masked their faces. Everything about Aminar, from her movements to her demeanor to her attire, seemed to announce "royalty," and Qui-Gon Jinn was not a fan of royalty. But he was on a mission, and he would do what was asked unless it crossed lines he had long before sworn never to cross.

"Ah, Qui-Gon Jinn, your expedience is appreciated," Aminar said, stepping closer, her smile forced and a bit weary. "Please relay our admiration to the Jedi Council."

Qui-Gon nodded.

"I thank you for the kind sentiment, Prefect," Qui-Gon said. "But I am here to find the child, nothing more."

The child.

"Ah, yes, all business. How charming you are," Aminar said, waving her arm as one would to dismiss a toddler throwing a tantrum. "Now, where is your own Padawan? Don't Jedi Knights often come in pairs?"

Qui-Gon forced a smile.

"My apprentice, Obi-Wan, is doing what he needs to do," Qui-Gon said, looking past the prefect and trying to see what lay beyond the hangar. "Focusing on his studies. He has much to learn. I am here at the behest of the Council and hope to return to Coruscant to continue training him as soon as possible."

Aminar started to speak, but Qui-Gon continued.

"Let us make haste, please," he said, motioning toward the hallway. "I have many questions and little time."

"We are at our lowest point, Qui-Gon Jinn," Aminar said as she brought a large golden goblet to her dark-red lips. She took a long pull before speaking again. "The makeshift forces of my rivals have united to form a powerful confederacy of armies—all with their sights set on my head. They claim to be for freedom, to sway my people. But they speak nothing close to the truth."

Qui-Gon didn't move. He was a patient man, but even so, this woman was challenging him. He was not there to learn about the planet's broken politics, nor was he there to help them solve their generations of chaos.

"With all due respect, Prefect Aminar, I believe it bears repeating—I am here to find the child," Qui-Gon said, his tone firm but patient. "A Padawan has been kidnapped by people claiming to be on this planet. You have informed the Jedi Council that you know where they have her hidden. Once I have that information, I will be on my way."

"Ah, so no time for small talk, then? No time to get to know your hosts?" Aminar said, tilting her head slightly, as if to get a better look at Qui-Gon. Her attendees, about a half-dozen cloaked figures, seemed to rustle at her tone. She was annoyed. "All business. I should have guessed. I realized the Jedi didn't like to get their robes dirty, but I hadn't experienced it firsthand."

Qui-Gon didn't respond. He'd learned long before that battles for the last word often resulted in defeat for both sides.

After a moment, Aminar motioned to one of the cloaked figures nearest her, who handed her a small datapad. She tapped a few buttons. A holographic map appeared, hovering over the tablet. It appeared to Qui-Gon to be a frigid, desolate terrain.

"Very well, I can play this your way," she said, handing the datapad to Qui-Gon. "This is where the

Dan'Gar forces have set up shop, a few territories from here, the capital. Abbott, my best pilot, will take you there. They are a massive army, and that is where your youngling is. Most probably, against her wishes."

Qui-Gon took a moment to scan the details that accompanied the visual. He could be there by night-fall, he reasoned. If he left now.

Don't overthink it. Don't wonder what it means.

Mace Windu had been right. Qui-Gon would certainly overthink this—the *why* of it all—if he lingered too long. But something else nagged at him, too. He would meditate on it as he journeyed to meet the Dan'Gar coalition.

Qui-Gon handed the tablet back to Aminar and took a step away, bowing slightly.

"Thank you for your help, Prefect Aminar. The Council will remember this," Qui-Gon said. "If that will be all, I—"

Aminar raised a hand.

"That will not be all, Qui-Gon Jinn," she said, her

eyes narrowing. "There is one more thing. And it has to be said, because I believe firmly in leaving nothing to chance. The Council will not only remember this, they will consider it a favor that needs to be repaid. Am I understood?"

Qui-Gon's left eyebrow shot up for a second, his reflex speeding past his conditioning. Prefect Aminar's hubris was strong—and worrisome.

"Understanding is not acceptance, Prefect," Qui-Gon said as he spun around, not waiting for a response. "It would serve you well to know that."

Qui-Gon sat alone in the rear cabin of the transport ship Aminar had loaned him. The pilot, the woman named Abbott, had been friendly enough as Qui-Gon boarded but also wary. This had not been a welcome assignment. This entire expedition was troublesome to all, it seemed.

He closed his eyes and visualized what was to come. The Council had been adamant that Qui-Gon be the envoy on this mission, and the reasons why were not yet clear to him. An errant Padawan named Lizel Liit had ended up there; that they knew. But had she departed of her own free will? Was she ensconced with these Desintian rebels by choice? Or had something else happened? None of the possible answers were good, Qui-Gon knew, but the result would have to be the same. Qui-Gon had to find the girl and take her home to Coruscant to face whatever discipline the Council determined.

But Qui-Gon also knew he was not chosen at random for this mission. The Council did not operate in a vacuum. They were well aware of Qui-Gon's own issues with the Jedi as a whole, and with his past. While Qui-Gon was optimistic about his apprentice, he was also wary of the process—for he had been burned by loss. The loss of his master. The tearing down of a relationship meant to be closer than blood. Could someone like Qui-Gon, who'd lost his strongest anchor to the Jedi teachings, save another, younger hopeful?

Qui-Gon opened his eyes as he felt the ship touch down. The time for those thoughts would come, he told himself. For now, he had a task to complete, and it would not be an easy one.

He stood up slowly, sliding his lightsaber into the right pocket of his robes. He stretched his arms and took in a series of long deep breaths. He turned at the sound of footsteps. It was Abbott. He'd protested against a chaperone but also knew he could press only so hard. Abbott was a stoic woman, her red hair tied back tightly, revealing a pale face with sharp feline features. Her voice was terse and direct.

"We are as close as I can bring you," she said, looking up at Qui-Gon. "Though we have no standing treaties with the rebels—Prefect Aminar refuses to recognize them—we do have an understanding. If a border existed, it would be a few kilometers from here."

Qui-Gon gave Abbott a wry smile.

"I'm well versed in the ways of factions and civil war," he said. "How will I contact their leader?"

Abbott licked her lips nervously before responding.

"They are aware that . . . someone is coming," she said.

Qui-Gon leaned forward slightly. He didn't like that response. No one would.

"What, exactly, has been communicated to the Dan'Gar?" he asked. He chided himself. He should have checked this all out long before landing on Desinta. He was distracted. He should be heeding Mace Windu's advice, he thought. "Who are they expecting?"

Abbott shrugged.

"Forgive me, Jedi, I am just a messenger," she said. "A go-between. My one job was to make sure you landed here safely and—"

"Then you have another, newer job," Qui-Gon

said, gingerly pulling out his lightsaber and looking it over, then watching her eyes as they scanned the deactivated weapon. "You will accompany me to meet the Dan'Gar. You will be my guide."

Abbott sputtered, her tough veneer cracked.

"That's—well, no, that's not acceptable. Aminar said—"

"I'm sure you've realized by now," Qui-Gon said with a humorless smile, "I don't care what Prefect Aminar says."

After a brief delay that involved Abbott complaining incessantly as she bundled up to step outside the tiny cruiser, they were on their way.

The snow that covered the ground was thick and hard, the top centimeter or so frozen from a storm the night before. They sloshed and crunched their way for a couple of kilometers before Abbott raised a hand, signaling for Qui-Gon to slow down. He could see nothing in any direction for long stretches, but somehow this woman knew exactly where they were. He had made the right choice in bringing her along, he thought.

"Here," she said. All he could see was her mouth. Her eyes were covered by a gigantic visor, her body bundled in a woolly coat and scarves. The wind was picking up, obscuring Qui-Gon's vision beyond her figure. "They're coming."

His lightsaber was out and active before she could pull her blaster completely from its holster. He sliced the weapon in half before she could get a shot off, the pieces falling silently, melting paths down into the aging snow. She lunged at Qui-Gon, but he sidestepped her, watching as she fell into the snow behind him. He swiveled around, lightsaber up, and waited.

She got up slowly. The wind was loud, but he thought he heard her emit a low groan. He let her get to her knees. Her hood was back, her red hair speckled with white. Her movements were resigned, understated. A soldier forced into a battle she knew she wouldn't win.

"What gave me away?"

Qui-Gon turned off his lightsaber and spoke, his voice louder as the winds picked up. "Your frustration at accompanying me," he said. "It felt too strong. Too definitive. It confirmed my suspicion."

"That this was a setup?" Abbott said, basically yelling across the short distance between them. "Good for you, Jedi. You made my job harder, but that's fine. The plan holds."

"Does it?" Qui-Gon asked.

"I've lied about all I've told you, Jedi," Abbott said. Even through the snow, Qui-Gon could see Abbott was smiling. "Except one thing."

Qui-Gon didn't ask. He didn't like word games.

Then Abbott spoke, her voice a low whisper.

"They're coming."

They came, riding fathiers, wielding axes and spears. About a dozen men, garbed in animal skins and dented armor, hooting and hollering as they approached Qui-Gon and Abbott. But for every piece of them that seemed from another time, modernities also appeared. Blasters. Cybernetic enhancements. Droids. These were not wild barbarians looking to derail civilization. This was an organized fighting force with the means to do some serious damage.

Qui-Gon knew the odds were against him even before he began to wield his weapon again, parrying attacks from the fathier-riding soldiers and keeping his flank protected from Abbott and anyone who circled around. He held on as long as he could—even knocking a few overconfident warriors off their steeds before the inevitable happened.

After the riders had taken turns coming at him, they regrouped, encircling Qui-Gon and running at him from all sides. Abbott lay nearby, curled in a ball after taking an elbow to the head. He didn't relish violence, but he couldn't say he hadn't taken some slight pleasure in disabling her. But it'd been a minor victory in a battle that was sure to end in his defeat, if not death.

Qui-Gon could feel and hear the fathiers' hooves turning the hardened snow into slush around him. Could see their muscled bodies coordinate their movements. Qui-Gon tried to remain calm, to make it seem like this was nothing, but he already knew it was over. It was just a matter of how—and when.

"We don't need an answer now, at this moment. But we do need one. And we know what you've been through. We understand what happened. Dooku's decision didn't affect just you, Qui-Gon."

Qui-Gon shook Mace Windu's advice away, trying to focus on what was happening—as the riders trotted closer to him, their voices rising, the whipping of their axes and the blaster fire creating an orchestra of war that felt at times unsettling and strangely invigorating.

Wasn't this what he lived for, Qui-Gon wondered. To fight? To defend the Jedi beliefs? Or was this just another petty skirmish in a galaxy of quibbles and wars? Even worse—was this just a sad, forgettable way to die?

For a brief moment, after Qui-Gon charged forward, lightsaber held high over his head, he thought he had a chance. He whispered an apology as he sliced at the regal creature in front of him, causing its rider to be tossed forward. Heavy breathing. Behind him. He couldn't turn around, though—not now. *Abbott.*

He thought he'd heard a sound—metal on metal—seconds before the blaster fire connected with his back, the pain spreading like fire over him. He fell to the snow, watching as his lightsaber shut off in midair and landed just out of his reach.

Then his vision went black.

"Wake up, please. Wake up."

Qui-Gon's eyes opened, slowly, as if even that simple movement would send him into spasms of pain.

It was dark. He could make that out, even though his vision remained blurry. And it was cold. He was shivering.

He heard rustling around him. Even in the darkness, he knew he was in a cramped, tight space. The one flicker of light wasn't a light at all, but a glimmer of a fire outside. Something meant to keep others warm. The rustling grew louder, and Qui-Gon felt a hand at his neck, guiding him up. Then something pressed to his lips.

"Here, drink this," someone said. It was a woman—no, a girl. A familiar voice.

He took a quick sip and licked his lips. He spoke, his voice a scratchy croak.

"Lizel," he said. "Lizel Liit. Is that you?"

"Yes," the girl said. He could make out her shape, and he thought he saw it shrink a bit as she spoke.

Shame was a powerful feeling, Qui-Gon realized. "I'm here."

Qui-Gon sat up, his back aching as he did so. He winced with each movement, but also felt some gratitude that he wasn't dead, and that the blaster had been set to stun. Apparently the Dan'Gar had bigger plans for the growing collection of Jedi prisoners.

"Tell me what you know," Qui-Gon said.

Even in the darkness, Qui-Gon could see the girl frown—her long brown hair framing her gray eyes and thin mouth. She hesitated a moment before speaking.

"I am—I just want to say how sorry I am, Master Qui-Gon, for you having to come—"

"Tell me what you know, Lizel," Qui-Gon said. "Not what you feel."

Lizel nodded to herself.

"I made a mistake," she started, her words halting at first, then growing more confident. "I needed some space. As a young Padawan, it felt like becoming a Jedi Knight was all I could ever want—the highest honor I could ever think to achieve. But, but as I grew older—I, well, I just wanted something else. To feel something different. I wasn't sure if I was good enough, Master. If I deserved to be what I was told I would be. I'm sure none of this makes sense."

Qui-Gon reached out a hand and found hers. He felt a charge of something as she clutched at his fingers. "So you ran," he said.

"I meant to tell my master—I should have," Lizel continued. "But I felt something . . . drawing me away. Something nudging me along to leave. Next thing I knew, I was on a spice-running ship headed for the Outer Rim. The pilot, a woman named Zarah Bliss, seemed to know where to go. She wanted to help me, or so I thought. Instead, she brought me here—and sold me to the highest bidder."

"The Dan'Gar?" Qui-Gon said. "It seems this planet is much more than a few small warring factions."

"Prefect Aminar is a savvy politician," Lizel said,

wiping a tear from her eye. "She knows that even though she may be at war with her own people, it is only through dueling alliances that she can remain in power."

"So when she heard one of her competitors had a Jedi Padawan, she thought she could help them double their winnings," Qui-Gon mused aloud. His head was throbbing, but he was slowly feeling better. "Was that it?"

Lizel shrugged.

"I suppose," she said. "They thought I was of value, but not much. But to have an actual Jedi Master? That was something of note. Something someone in power would want."

Qui-Gon straightened up and placed a hand on Lizel's tiny shoulder.

"That was a foolish mistake on their part. A mistake born of hubris and ignorance," he said. "You made one, as well—but yours was a natural one. We all must question what's asked of us from time to time.

Those who follow blindly are bound to trip and fall."

Lizel's eyes widened in surprise.

"Are you sure, Master? Do you ever question the Jedi ways?" she asked. "It all feels so . . . predetermined. I felt like I'd failed my future self."

Qui-Gon scoffed.

"Questioning is in itself the Jedi way," he said. "Don't let anyone tell you otherwise."

"We need you on the Council, Qui-Gon. We need your wisdom. Dooku was lost. Something pulled him away. We need you by our side, my friend."

Qui-Gon grimaced at the memory. At the decision that still weighed on him.

Had they sent him there—to save this errant Padawan—because he had yet to say yay or nay? Because they wanted to test him? Perhaps, Qui-Gon thought. But that wouldn't change his current reality. Or what needed to be done.

"Are you all right, Master?"

"I will be better shortly," he said, lying back down

on the stone cot. "Now, come closer, youngling—and listen very carefully."

"He's gone. Oh dear, oh dear—he's dead!"

Lizel's scream burst out of the small cell, echoing down the halls of their jail. Footsteps hurried toward the room.

A guard, cloaked in green and holding a large blaster in one hand, approached the bars that separated Lizel and Qui-Gon from freedom. He peered into the cell and seemed to notice that Qui-Gon wasn't moving.

"What's going on here?"

"He started shaking—spasming," Lizel said, her voice panicked and almost hysterical. "I, uh, I tried to calm him—but then he just stopped. And he's not moving. I think he's dead. He's dead. Is that possible?"

The jangling of keys. The creak of metal as the door opened. Then the guard was inside, his large figure looming over Lizel and the prone Qui-Gon.

"Jedi are just people, foolish child. Did you learn nothing by their side?" the gruff guard said. "But this one is of no use to us dead."

He reached for Qui-Gon, as if to shake him, but the Jedi's eyes opened immediately.

The guard stepped back, surprised. "What is this trickery?"

Qui-Gon sat up with a speed and grace that seemed to surprise even Lizel. He moved his hand outward, as if tapping the air in front of the guard. Almost immediately, the thug was sent hurtling across the tiny room, his head banging against the cinder wall. By the time the jailer's body slid down to the ground, Qui-Gon was standing.

"No trickery," Qui-Gon said flatly. "I promise you."

"You . . . you did that," she sputtered. "The Force . . . Your mastery of it . . ."

He looked at Lizel and nodded.

"We can talk about it later," he said. "But now we run."

He found his lightsaber nearby, tucked away haphazardly in what seemed like a storage area, in a pile of discarded blasters and other weapons. Qui-Gon would have taken offense if he'd had the time.

The prison seemed desolate as Qui-Gon led Lizel down what appeared to be the main hallway. He could see the snow billowing wildly outside. Qui-Gon tried not to worry about how they'd get back to his ship. Not yet.

They caught a pair of guards a few meters away, at a small station near a juncture. Qui-Gon disabled them with a look as he activated his lightsaber. Neither was armed. Neither was willing to die, either.

"Take us to Abbott," Qui-Gon said. "Now."

Qui-Gon heard Aminar's voice before he entered her chamber. He tried his best not to smile.

"Abbott? You're here? What is the meaning of this?"

The slight gasp that came from Aminar's mouth as she saw him and Lizel enter was an added bonus, Qui-Gon thought.

"Qui-Gon, why, what a—a pleasant surprise," the prefect said, modifying her tone immediately, trying to match her circumstances with a cunning precision that impressed and irked Qui-Gon in equal measure. "I had heard rumblings that you'd been captured— hurt, even."

"The rumors of my defeat were just that, Prefect Aminar," Qui-Gon said. He could feel Lizel behind him, cautiously keeping pace. "But something tells me you were kept abreast of my whereabouts with little delay."

"Why, I have no idea what you're implying, Jedi," Aminar said, incredulous. "I opened my doors to you and allowed you passage to find your errant youngling—which it seems you have."

"Your assistant says otherwise," Qui-Gon said, motioning toward Abbott, who'd backed away, as if trying to blend into the ornate wall opposite Aminar. "So I will ask you to put aside the misdirection and speak plainly, or not speak at all."

Silence hung between them for a long moment before Aminar spoke again.

"I know defeat when I see it, Qui-Gon Jinn," she said carefully. "Let us part quickly and with some dignity, no? Your ship is docked where you left it. I promise you I will not threaten your exit. You cannot fault me for trying, can you? There are few things as rare as a Jedi prisoner. If it could help bring peace to my world, I was bound to see it through."

Qui-Gon motioned for Lizel to make her way toward the ship. The young Padawan complied, eager to leave the room. Abbott followed, but her progress was frozen when Qui-Gon spoke.

"Blame and fault are not relevant here, Prefect," Qui-Gon said. "But it does rest squarely on your shoulders, nonetheless. My only hope is that you've learned not to make the same mistake twice."

Aminar's nose seemed to scrunch up at Qui-Gon's words. He'd gotten past her defensive posture—tapping into something she held quite dear. Her ego.

"Is that a threat, Jedi? How quaint," she said, a dry laugh escaping her lips. "Much stronger, deadlier men have said worse. I will not lose a second of sleep over this—or your escape. Now, be gone. I miscalculated. A rarity, I assure you. But I have a planet to govern and much more important things to deal with than an aging Jedi Master's obtuse lectures."

Qui-Gon nodded knowingly.

"That you do, that you do," he said before turning toward the door that led to the docking area. Prefect Aminar cleared her throat nervously.

"What does that mean?" she asked. "Another empty threat?"

Her voice rose with each word—a mix of hubris and fear, Qui-Gon thought.

"Not empty, no," he said. "You spoke much truth

just now. You do have more important things to deal with. I would say about three hundred more."

"Three hundred?"

"That's the number of Dan'Gar men that accompanied me back here, thirsty for their own brand of vengeance," Qui-Gon said. "They seemed quite upset by your antics. I'm not sure your usual method of politicking will work as well this time around."

Qui-Gon didn't wait for her to respond. The sound of her harried, panicked words was muted by the door that closed behind him.

"Will they take me back?"

Lizel's question hung between them. Qui-Gon was in the pilot's seat of his small ship, with Lizel seated to his right, a deep questioning look in her young eyes. Qui-Gon wished he could answer her with something definitive, something soothing. But the galaxy wasn't built that way.

"I cannot predict what the Council will do," Qui-Gon said, looking out toward the stars. "But I do believe that indecision and uncertainty from someone so young should not disqualify them from returning. We do not all know our paths so early in life."

He didn't need to see Lizel placing her head in her hands to know she was crying. Softly, but crying. She tried to muffle the sound of her tears, but it was too late. After a few moments Lizel let herself sob completely.

Qui-Gon gently placed a hand on her shoulder, and her whimpering quieted.

"I once knew someone, a teacher, a mentor," Qui-Gon said. "Someone who I looked to as my guide in all things. He made a choice—he did something that I couldn't fathom. It created a feeling inside me. A doubt and fear that I never thought I could overcome. I was lost for a good while. Shaken to my core."

Lizel wiped at her eyes as Qui-Gon continued.

"But over time, that fear and doubt became something else—it became resolve. A feeling of understanding and confidence—in myself and what I was capable of," Qui-Gon said. "It would have been normal to resent him. To blame this other person's decisions for whatever errors I made. But that would also have been the easy path, a lazy and passive one."

"So . . . what did you do?" Lizel asked. "What do I do?"

Qui-Gon turned to face the child. He looked into her eyes—he saw youth, fear, insecurity, and rebellion. But he also saw hope—and strength.

"I trusted myself. I worked harder. I accepted that one man's mistakes would never carry the weight of my own," Qui-Gon said. "I studied the Jedi teachings. I interpreted them as best I could. And I listened and learned. We are all flawed, Lizel. We all make errors of judgment. It's how we recover from them that defines us."

Lizel nodded. She let out a long breath and placed her hand on Qui-Gon's shoulder. He looked over at the young Padawan.

She returned his gaze for what felt like the first time, a grateful smile brightening her face. Qui-Gon responded in kind.

THE EYE OF THE BEHOLDER

SARWAT CHADDA

THE GARDENS OF DEVALOK burned. The great huluppu trees lit the horizon in gold and crimson, filling the air with the perfume of their wood. Vast clouds of fiery ash danced in the scented breeze. Zohra never imagined the end of the world would smell so sweet, or look so beautiful?

They'd said war wouldn't come to Devalok. Zohra remembered her parents and their friends debating back and forth all the reasons why they were safe. The planet had no . . . what was the word? *Strategic*? Yes, the planet had no strategic value. It was far away from the politics of Coruscant, and what did it produce? Nothing but gardeners! They were no danger to the Separatists and no help to the Republic.

They'd all said they were safe.

They'd all been wrong, and now the gardens burned.

"When are they coming?" whined Dumuz.

"Soon."

"You said that yesterday! And the day before! When, Zohra? When?" He stomped around the room, emphasizing each outburst. "When? When? When?"

"Shh! Shh! They'll hear us!"

A clanking patrol had only just gone down their street an hour earlier.

"When? When? When?"

"Dumuz! Stop it!" Why wouldn't he listen? Why didn't he understand? "That's enough!"

The roar of the fighter overhead shook the whole building. The few remaining windows rattled in their frames. Then there was a high-pitched scream as the missiles were fired. She hated that sound more than anything. A few moments later the city echoed with a distant explosion.

Dumuz stared, open-mouthed, at the window as the sky flickered with fresh fire. "Where did it go? What did it hit?"

The fumes from the fighter's engines filled the narrow street, and Zohra covered her mouth as she peered through the gap in one of the boarded-up windows.

Great black clouds billowed up from the west. What was west? What had still been left standing? Some government building? The old palace? Were the greenhouses to the west? No, please not the greenhouses.

"What did it hit?" said Dumuz, coughing.

"It doesn't matter anymore. Cover your mouth."

He looked up at her. "My throat's so dry, Zohra. I'm *thirsty*."

Zohra licked her own dry lips. "Take some water. Half a cup. Only half a cup, got it?"

He nodded miserably and did as he was told. Zohra tried to ignore the sound of the water pouring from the jug and sloshing in the cup. She didn't need to drink. She could wait. They needed to make it last. Water was precious.

It hadn't been. It had flowed freely across the city. Along canals, from fountains, from the vast mist towers that watered the parades of plants on every street. From the sky.

Now all that fell was fire and death.

Dumuz sat cross-legged in the middle of the room, gazing empty-eyed at his empty cup. "I drank it too quickly. It's all gone now."

They'd shut off the water to the building in the first week. They'd all gone to the fountain to refill their bottles. Then the droids had demolished the fountain with a single shot from their cannon. Why? Droids didn't drink. Maybe they thought no one else needed to, either.

"Have another half," she said.

He didn't need to be told twice. "What about you?"

She watched the water pour from the jug. How it sparkled. "I'm not thirsty."

Water, food, and silence. That's what Dad had said would get them through the siege. The Republic would come. They would be saved. They had a vast army with the best, bravest warriors in all the galaxy. They had the Jedi.

Mom had studied in Coruscant. She'd shown them holoimages of the Jedi Temple. She'd worked a year in their garden and seen Master Yoda, sitting amongst the flowers. Her mom had been too frightened to say anything to him, and regretted it ever since.

Zohra would have spoken to him. She would have hidden behind the bushes to watch Master Windu train. She would have explored the library and spoken to the Jedi scholars. Learned their tales and all their stories.

Their stories . . .

Zohra sat down beside her brother. "Do you want a story?"

He gazed around their darkened home glumly. "There's no power. The datapads don't work anymore."

Zohra squeezed him. "You think I don't know them all by heart by now? I've heard them a million times."

"A billion!" he shouted. "A billion billion!"

"Shhh! Shhh!"

He winced and put his finger to his lips, but oh, how he grinned.

That grin. It burst from him, and suddenly the whole room seemed brighter. She needed to remind herself he was only six.

"Which one do you want to hear first?" she said. "How about when the Jedi Master Uma Kalidi defeated the entire army of the fear-naughts by herself and saved all of Devalok?"

"Uma! Uma! Uma!" chanted Dumuz, clapping softly.

Who didn't love stories about Uma Kalidi? The famous Jedi had been born on Devalok, and every schoolkid knew all about her. Zohra had dressed up as her for the Blossom Festival, like every other kid. Dad had even made her a toy lightsaber. The blade, harmless and flickering, had shone green instead of blue, but it had been close enough and made her the envy of the whole parade. And yeah, she'd spent the night trying to use the Force to summon it from the table across her bedroom. Like every other kid *ever*.

What had happened to that lightsaber?

She'd grown up, that's what. She'd gotten too old for fairy tales.

Not Dumuz. He gazed up at her, eyes wide and bright with expectation.

Where to begin? Where else but the beginning? "Once upon a time in a galaxy we call our own, there was a gardener called Uma. All the plants and flowers she tended grew taller, brighter, and more perfumed than anyone else's. You see, Uma had a special, magical power."

"The Force," whispered Dumuz. "Go to the bit when she fights the bounty hunters! With her lightsaber! I want all the noises, too!"

"That's not till much later, you know that."

"I want the fighting!" He jumped up and grabbed his thumb, pretending it was his own lightsaber. "*Fruuummmm . . . kish! Kish! Kish!* Look at me, Zohra! *Frummm!* I'd slice the droids into scrap! One Jedi could beat the whole droid army! Like this!" He thrust out his hand. "Knock them all into the sea!"

"Hey, do you want my story, or are you making up one of your own?"

Dumuz struck a proud pose. "Jedi Master Dumuz of Devalok."

Zohra collapsed against the sofa. "Oh, brave Jedi Master! Please help me! There are monsters coming to eat me!"

Dumuz jumped up and down on the cushions. "*Frummmm! Fruuum! Fruuum!* There! All the monsters are dead! The Force is with me!"

"Thank you, Master Jedi! I don't know what—"

"Roger, roger."

Footsteps clanked in the stone hallway; the buzz

of motorized joints echoed along the corridor, getting closer.

"Check the apartments for survivors."

"Roger, roger."

Zohra bit down a scream as the blasters opened up. Doors, walls, windows were blown away, and the droids began their sweep through the building.

Had they heard them playing? They should have been more careful! She'd just wanted to make Dumuz happy, just for a short while, but that weakness had put them in danger.

Holding Dumuz tightly, Zohra crept toward the cupboard. She froze when the hinges creaked, but the droids were busy destroying the apartments across the corridor. Dumuz squeezed himself against the pipes and ducts of the apartment's environmental system. Zohra crawled in against him and closed the cupboard door as quietly as she could.

The apartment shook as the front doors were blasted open. The smell of smoke and burning metal filled the small apartment as, through the minute gap where the cupboard door didn't quite meet the frame, she watched the droids march in.

She'd never seen them so close.

They looked like insects, spindly but deadly. It was dark. Dad had boarded up the windows the moment the invasion had begun, but there were enough gaps through the cracks in the wall for the ash-filtered sunlight to cast a red hue over the room, and its intruders. One droid approached the water container and tipped it over with its foot, letting it gurgle out over the wooden floor. Another found the neat bags of fruit, rice, and nourish-paste, and flattened it all with the butt of its blaster. The third explored the rest of the house while the fourth, a commander, stood in the center of the room, turning its long metal snout from side to side.

Zohra willed her heart to stop beating.

Could it hear them? Could it smell them?

"Switching to infrared."

"Roger, roger."

Being alive betrayed them.

She screamed as the droid tore the door off and grabbed her by the hair. It pulled her out and across the floor.

"Let her go!" yelled Dumuz, kicking hopelessly against the other droid, who had him in its arms. It hauled him into the middle of the room and dropped him beside Zohra.

The two droids stood over them, blasters poised. "Look like dangerous rebels, sir."

"Standard elimination protocol," replied the commander.

"Roger, roger."

She didn't beg. She didn't plead for their lives. She wasn't afraid, not right then. She felt her brother's breath on her neck as he nuzzled against her, hiding his eyes from that terrible brief moment when the blasters would flash and all would end. The commander lowered his blaster so it was centimeters from her face. She felt the heat from the barrel.

The droid began shaking. The gears within the droid's mechanisms groaned, then shrieked as they crumpled against each other. The metal head buckled and erupted into flame.

A sudden intense light filled the small room, along with a deep vibrating hum. Fresh shadows rose across the walls and the ceiling, and a figure stood in the doorway, a black silhouette of a man wielding a beam of fearsome blue.

The second droid turned and fired. It couldn't miss at such a short range. The noise was deafening.

The man swept the blue beam in front of him. Zohra blinked as the room flared with the blinding light of the impact of the blaster shot against it, and then the man turned the blue beam with a twist of his wrist and separated the droid's torso from its hips and flicked once more, slicing the head from its neck. All in a single eyeblink.

"To your left, Anakin!" snapped a second man, just as the droid that had been exploring the other rooms burst back into the corridor. This second man, older than the first and bearded, swung his own brilliant blue blade as the droid fired, and the blaster bolt bounced off the blade into the ceiling. The bearded man rammed the blade straight through the droid's core, then brought it out with a twist, tearing the droid wide open.

They struck the fourth, final droid simultaneously. The younger swapped the blade to his opposite hand and struck high, with the bearded man, taking a double grip, swiping low across the waist. The droid clattered to the floor in three smoldering pieces.

The younger man crouched down and held out a gloved hand. "Are you hurt?"

Zohra couldn't speak. She couldn't think. Was it

shock? Relief? Just confusion? How could the world be turned upside down in so few seconds?

The young man winced. "Oh, sorry." He deactivated his weapon, and the beam instantly vanished. His older companion, standing by the door watching them, did the same and hooked the weapon to his belt.

She knew exactly what the weapon was. She gazed at it, then at the young man smiling gently at her. "Who are you?"

That gentleness warmed his blue eyes. "I'm Anakin Skywalker."

"Did Mom and Dad send you?" Dumuz rushed up to him. "They must have! I knew it, see, Zohra? I knew it!"

Anakin straightened the water canister. There was no point, but he put it back on the stool. "How long have you been here by yourselves?"

"Five days, Master Jedi." What else could he be?

He laughed as he shook his head. "There's only one Master here, and that's him. Meet Master Obi-Wan Kenobi. I'm just Anakin. How about you?"

"This is Dumuz, and I'm Zohra. We've been here five days . . . Anakin. Mom and Dad went out to get supplies. They said they'd be back. We're still waiting."

Obi-Wan pushed a smile onto his lips. Zohra knew what it meant; she'd seen all the grown-ups wear that kind of smile more and more as things got worse and worse. "Tell me, youngling, how long are they usually away for?"

"Only a few hours."

She needed to be strong even though she'd never felt weaker in her whole life. It was as if she was standing on a branch at a great height and it was starting to bend. Would she fall? If she did, there would be no one there to catch her, not anymore.

Obi-Wan drew his hand over his beard as he met her gaze. "Let's go find them, shall we?"

"Where are we going?" Zohra asked.

Obi-Wan held up a small holodisplay. Zohra could see that it was the city, or at least the northern district. "Amrit spaceport. It's still held by the Republic, but not for much longer. We need to be quick."

Dumuz looked up at him. "And that's where Mom and Dad will be?"

Anakin avoided the question and instead gestured to the other rooms. "Is there anything you want to take?"

Dumuz nodded. "My Wookiee! I can't leave him!"

"Then go get him," said Anakin. "How about you, Zohra?"

Zohra shook her head. "Nothing."

Nothing at all. It had stopped feeling like home a long time ago.

Obi Wan gestured with his holodisplay. "The evacuation route's marked, Anakin. We should—"

"Will you help us?" asked Anakin. "To get through the city?"

Why were they asking her? Jedi didn't need help;

they could do everything. Anything. But Zohra looked at the holodisplay. "That route's for vehicles. There's another way to the spaceport, along the old canal and the factories. They closed down ages ago. No one uses that way anymore."

Obi-Wan frowned, but nodded. "The droids won't be able to get their tanks along the canal, but it'll take longer. How well do you know the canals?"

"Mom is head gardener at Enki greenhouse. She's in charge of turning the factories into new gardens. We go there plenty."

"The canal then."

Dumuz rushed back, clutching Fuzzy. "I found him."

Anakin scratched the toy's woolly chin. "He looks fierce."

"He is. He looks after me when I sleep. Are we going now?"

Zohra took her brother's hand. It was her job to look after him.

Obi-Wan looked both ways along the corridor, his hand resting on the lightsaber hilt. "Follow me."

They'd demolished the old fountain. It had been the heart of the neighborhood, the five main avenues all radiating from it. That was where the local park was, where they'd splash around on hot days and climb the statues.

Now it was just rubble and dust. "Why?"

Obi-Wan pointed down one of the avenues. "It was blocking the view. From here you have a clear line of fire in all directions."

They'd even ripped up Old Granny, the oldest tree in the neighborhood and the one with the lowest branches. Every kid had learned how to climb with the help of Old Granny.

She tightened her grip on Dumuz. He gazed silently at the burnt remains of the park, of the rocking banthas that were just molten slag. The small paddling pool was empty but for a bundle of clothes someone had thrown in. Why would . . . ?

Zohra turned Dumuz away. He didn't need to see what—who—was in the pool.

"I'm going to tell Mom and Dad off for leaving us for so long. They should have told us." Dumuz suddenly grinned. "I didn't know they were friends with Jedi! Isn't that amazing, Zohra?"

"Yeah, amazing."

"It'll be good to see them, won't it?" he asked, his voice faltering. "See that they're safe and sound and nothing bad happened to them?"

Zohra didn't know what to say so said nothing. Dumuz tugged her hand. "They're safe and sound, aren't they?"

Why did he keep asking? What did he want her to say? Five days! Didn't he know what that meant?

"Here, try this."

It was Anakin. He'd fallen a few paces behind Obi-Wan to join them. He held out a chewy stick.

"Don't ask me what it's made of. Probably better not knowing the truth."

Zohra took it and broke it in half, giving Dumuz the bigger half. It didn't taste of anything, but her stomach still growled. Dumuz laughed, which was better than him asking questions. Then he tugged her, pointing at Anakin. "Look at his hand."

The right sleeve of his tunic was torn, revealing the gears and mechanisms of the robotic limb. Zohra frowned at her brother. "It's rude to point."

"He must be a great warrior," said Dumuz.

But Anakin heard. He looked over his shoulder, eyebrow arched. "But the other guy was better."

"But next time you'll win, won't you?"

It could have just been the smoke or the brief flicker of the firelight, but a shadow passed over Anakin's face. The warmth of him vanished, just like that. Then he winked, and the darkness was gone.

Flames floated upon the oily water of the Old Canal. The factories, which had long ago returned to nature, smoldered, and clouds of smoke hung low over their roofless shells.

Obi-Wan drew his comlink as they reached the first junction. "Commander Varna. This is General Kenobi. Come in, Commander."

The comlink crackled. "General Kenobi? We thought we'd lost you. Where are you? Is Skywalker with you?"

"We're both fine. How are you holding up?"

"Not good, truth be told. The droids are getting reinforcements and the blockade's getting tighter, not many ships getting through. We're due one last pickup, and then we're gone. We'll wait as long as we can."

"We've got some civilians with us. Could you arrange us a LAAT?"

"A larty? You'd be lucky." Varna sounded unsure and surprised. "I thought all the politicians and essential personnel had got out weeks ago."

"Just do what you can," said Obi-Wan.

"Yes, sir. Varna out."

Obi-Wan tucked away the comlink and peered ahead, his fingers drumming on his lightsaber hilt. "If we keep a good pace, we should reach the port within a few hours. The troopers will be able to last that long. You'll be safe then."

"Safe? Where's safe?" snapped Zohra. "Where are we going? Some refugee camp in the Outer Rim? I've heard the stories. People being abandoned on asteroids because they're not *essential* personnel, whatever that means. The Republic doesn't care about people like us, it never has."

"What about Mom and Dad?" said Dumuz. "I want them! Are they at the spaceport?"

Zohra pulled Dumuz hard. "They're not at the port. They're not anywhere. They're not waiting for us, and they're not coming back. They're *dead*, Dumuz. They are gone forever, and we're alone!"

There. She'd said it. The terrible truth that people died in wars. It didn't matter how much you loved someone; that wouldn't protect them. Wishes were meaningless, and the fairy tales were just that.

Dumuz stood there, silent, but with tears running down his sooty cheeks. He didn't argue, didn't fight, didn't attack her for hurting him. She wished he would. Zohra wanted to feel pain. Instead all she felt was hollow.

She crouched and pulled Dumuz against her. This is what she felt: His breath. His warmth. His tremors as he sobbed inside himself. Those tears of his upon her cheek. "But why can I still hear them, Zohra? I can hear them calling for us."

"I wish it was true, Dumuz." She wiped his tears and tried to smile. "We need to look out for one another, okay?"

"But I can hear them. I can. I know their voices."

Anakin turned to the two of them. "Tell me what you hear."

What was he doing? Giving Dumuz such false hope? It had been five days. . . .

Dumuz met the Jedi's gaze with a seriousness that was older than his mere six years. You grew up quickly in war. "They're together. They're tired, they're scared. They're calling us but are getting weak. I don't know what it means."

"Do you know where they went?" asked Anakin.

Zohra took Dumuz's hand. "The Enki greenhouse. Mom thought there might still be food in the vaults."

Obi-Wan shook his head. "They bombed Enki five days ago."

Anakin frowned. "We need to look."

"We'll be losing precious time, Anakin. Enki's on the front line, and we'll be on our own."

"What's new about that, Master?" Anakin turned back to Dumuz. "We need to trust our feelings."

They hid from the tanks, from the marching legions of the battle droids and the rattling clatter of the droidekas as they raced along the cratered highways.

As night fell the stars were replaced with silent, darting beams and explosions that blossomed in the darkness. Obi-Wan watched the display grimly through his monoculars. "The orbital blockade is tightening. I don't know how much longer the fleet can hold out. They'll have to jump to hyperspace soon to avoid being wiped out."

"They'll hold awhile longer," said Anakin stubbornly.

Zohra could barely lift her legs. Only the tight grip of Dumuz's little fingers on hers kept her going. But in the wrong direction. "Why are we doing this? Because of a feeling? Because of what Dumuz said? He's not a Jedi. He doesn't have the Force."

Obi-Wan gestured to them both. "He does. So do you. So does every living thing. It's what binds the galaxy together. Each of us to the others. Sometimes you can hear the will of the Force, if you are quiet and willing to listen."

"Do you believe that?" asked Zohra.

"It's true," said Anakin. He had climbed one of the broken walls and stood silhouetted against the horizon fires. "Is that Enki?"

What had they done to it? This was where Zohra had come since she could remember, walking among the great plants and flowers gathered from all over the galaxy. She'd chased fluttering asabs with their beautiful patterned wings through the mist gardens and picnicked under the expansive boughs of the ancient huluppus. Now what remained? The frame of the vast greenhouse had been reduced to twisted slag, and the power fields flickered and crackled. Sparks still jumped between the power nodes, and the leaves upon the nearby trees smoldered.

And yet, it was not all ruin.

One huluppu tree remained. It made no sense why; all around it was devastation. It was grand, ancient beyond counting, and yet its branches swelled with silvery leaves, which shimmered like a galaxy of stars held within some great nebula. The hues changed with the breeze, with the erratic temperature of the heat-laden gusts.

They approached in somber silence. For a moment the war seemed far away. Anakin reached up and touched a leaf with his bare fingers. "Trees don't grow on Tatooine."

The rich, moist ground was covered in debris and ash. The massive ferns from Kashyyyk were nothing more than brittle blackened stalks.

Trees had fallen. Vast sections of the greenhouse had collapsed; the various buildings within, the laboratories, the classrooms and storerooms, were just piles of shattered stone and burnt wood. The air was arid and coated the back of her throat with a harsh, bitter taste.

Anakin picked up what looked like a large stone. He brushed off the coating of ash, exposing the yellow skin underneath. "What's this? It smells delicious."

"A huluppu fruit," said Zohra. "I thought the season was over."

Anakin sliced it open with his robotic fingertip. The smell rose thickly from the moist flesh beneath the skin. Anakin quartered it neatly and handed it out.

Her hands shook as she took her slice. The juices dripped onto her fingers, sticky, delicious. She ate with her eyes closed. The taste belonged to better, sweeter times. When she opened her eyes, Anakin was nodding and even Obi-Wan was taking his time to savor the taste. Anakin handed Dumuz the fruit's seed. "Something for your garden."

A moment later Dumuz slipped from her and ran off into the undergrowth.

"Dumuz! Come back!"

They raced after him. The fire-blackened trunks still flickered with embers, and smoke still rose from the heaps of plants, and Dumuz, small as he was, darted through the wreckage quickly, nimbly. "Dumuz! Wait!"

Then they stumbled out into a large courtyard. Through the soot she could still make out the ancient mosaic of the tree of life, the legend of how the first huluppu tree had given birth to the galaxy, how its shiny leaves had become the stars and how the branches held up the sky. But most of the courtyard was just rubble. Dumuz stood among the pieces of broken mosaic. "Mom? Dad?"

Obi-Wan looked over at Anakin. "Well?"

Anakin climbed over the wreckage toward what would have been the entrance to the vaults. "I think you'd better stand back."

Zohra didn't understand. "There's no way into the vaults. There must be a hundred tonnes over the entrance."

"What does Master Yoda say?" Anakin closed his eyes and stretched out his fingers.

"Size matters not," answered Obi-Wan.

There was an eerie silence. Even the echoes of the explosions and blaster fire in the distance faded away. Peace fell over the courtyard as Anakin faced the mountain of wreckage before him.

What could he possibly do? It was asking the imposs—

The largest trunk creaked. The rubble scraped against itself. The broken pieces of mosaic shook and began to *rise*.

Dirt, dust, and ash swirled around Anakin as a crooked section of framework bent back on itself, clearing a path. The great chunks of stone rolled backward or rose over each other, drifting to the sides, where they stayed, suspended in the air.

The stones, the twisted metal, the burnt remains of the trees parted, and through them Zohra saw the buckled door to the vaults. It was many centimeters thick, sealed to avoid contaminants. Obi-Wan walked up to it, ignited his lightsaber, and in a single fluid stroke sliced the door in half. The heavy sections slammed to the ground, echoing loudly within the bare stone opening. The ground shook as Anakin dropped the rubble, and the dust took a few moments to settle. What was through the doors? Zohra, trembling with fear and hope, stepped closer. . . .

The light radiating from the humming blade glinted off the corners and edges of the metallic containers lining the walls. And fell upon the two figures slumped on the floor.

She couldn't believe it. This existed only in fairy tales but had happened right in front of her. Then she ran toward them. Obi-Wan crouched beside one figure, using his tunic to wipe their face clean. "Hello there."

The eyes fluttered, and suddenly, as the breeze blew away the stale vault air, the figure coughed. Zohra's mom looked around, bewildered but alive.

Dumuz screamed as he ran into their dad's arms. Zohra stared at her mom, her filthy palms pressed against her own cheeks, ignoring the tears running between her fingers.

Lights erupted from above them, bathing them in

an inescapable blinding beam. The drone of the engines grew deafening as the droid battle tank descended out of the darkness. The cannon swiveled to point directly at them.

The loudspeaker hummed to life. "Surrender now or we will open fire."

Zohra didn't even see Obi-Wan move. One moment he was kneeling beside her parents; the next he was running up the battle tank as it hovered fifteen meters above them. In the swirling smoke he ignited his lightsaber and slashed *through* the tank's cannon. The long metal cylinder clanged upon the hull, then tumbled to the ground.

"Get off the tank!" the voice boomed from the loudspeaker. "Get him off the tank!"

"Roger, roger!"

Hatches opened, light spilling from within as battle droids scuttled out even as the tank tilted from side to side, vainly trying to throw the Jedi off as he carved deep molten grooves through the hull.

The tree trunk beside Zohra began to move.

Anakin had his gaze locked on the tank while the trunk, ten meters long, aimed its sheared tip toward it. Anakin flicked his hand forward.

The engines erupted into flames and burning debris as the tree skewered the tank. Explosions rocked it from within, and a great gout of flames blew out from the open hatches. Two droids, still clambering out, disappeared in the sudden inferno.

Obi-Wan didn't linger as smoke poured from the devastated craft. He launched himself backward, turning in midair, and landed lightly back in the courtyard.

Up above them the tank spun out of control and rocked as the ammunition exploded. Droids tumbled from the disintegrating vehicle to smash apart upon the ruin of the greenhouse.

Anakin joined Obi-Wan. "It's not over yet."

More lights appeared through the dense smoke. The

ground shook as a host of spider droids approached, crossing the shattered terrain easily on their spindly legs. A line of battle tanks swiveled their turrets toward the greenhouse.

Obi-Wan scowled. "What did you do to upset them, Anakin?"

"Me? It's you who cause all the trouble. I'm just your humble *Padawan*, remember?"

"You? Humble?" snorted Obi-Wan. He winced as he saw the lights from behind. "Hmm. They're being remarkably thorough. I think we might have—"

Zohra screamed as a gunship swooped overhead, lacerating the night with blazing laser beams. Spider droids erupted, and the rest scuttled for cover.

The gunship's repulsor engines droned as it descended to hover over the courtyard. Clone troopers gathered at the hatches, one of them beckoning the little group forward. "Come on!"

"Commander Varna!" yelled Obi-Wan. "How good of you to join us!"

"I couldn't let you fellas have all the fun!"

One trooper swept Dumuz into his arms while another helped their mom and dad. Anakin gestured to her. "Time to leave, Zohra."

She had barely gotten on board before the gunship began its ascent. Anakin shoved her into a seat. She stared at Dumuz, beside her, and her parents opposite.

The Jedi had done this all for them. They weren't special, weren't essential personnel, but the Jedi still had risked it all, just for them.

The gunship trembled violently as a laser blast tore off one of the gun pods. Commander Varna hung off the open hatch. "The larty's coming under heavy fire! We need to take evasive—"

And then he was gone. There was a flash from below, the burst of sudden heat, and the commander disappeared.

Obi-Wan slapped Anakin's shoulder. "They've got us in a cross fire! We go any higher and we'll be obliterated!"

Anakin nodded, but as he turned toward the opening, he stopped and looked back at her. "Stay safe, Zohra."

What was he . . . ?

He was going back.

Anakin unhooked his lightsaber. The beam erupted from the hilt, and he joined Obi-Wan on the precipice while laser beams crisscrossed the darkness.

She needed to say something, to tell him what he'd done for them all, how he'd saved them. "Anakin!"

She couldn't get it all out, say all she wanted to say. But then there was a better way, one he'd truly understand. "May the Force be with you."

And then they jumped.

It was four hours to Naboo. The capital ship's vast docking bays had been converted into a campsite for the thousands of refugees the Republic had been able to evacuate. They were safe in hyperspace; they should be resting, but Zohra was wide awake. She sat on her sleeping bag, gazing at her parents, exhausted, asleep, safe. When she turned to Dumuz's bunk, he closed his eyes.

"Can't sleep, either, eh?" she said, snuggling in next to him.

He shook his head and squeezed his Wookiee. "What will we do, Zohra? Home's gone."

She put the huluppu seed in his hand. "Plant this somewhere. Make that our home."

He cradled it in his lap. "Can I have a story?"

Zohra leaned back against the hull. The engines thrummed softly against her, and the structure was warm. "Once upon a time, in a galaxy we call ours, there were two heroes. Their names were Obi-Wan Kenobi and Anakin Skywalker."

Dumuz snuggled against her as she wrapped her arm around him.

"They were the finders of lost children, tomb breakers, and"—her gaze fell upon the seed—"hope bringers." She closed her eyes. There they were. Anakin, his smile and his warmth, and Obi-Wan, formal but dedicated. "They were Jedi Knights, and one day they came to Devalok. . . ."

A JEDI'S DUTY

KAREN STRONG

BARRISS OFFEE SENSED a disturbance in the Force. The harrowing feeling was familiar, and the looming presence darkened her thoughts.

She opened her eyes to the surroundings of her room. A small statue of a Mirialan deity was on the altar in front of her. Several candles provided a warm glow against the bare walls, but their luminescence fluttered with her shallow breaths.

Barriss had failed at meditation yet again.

Although she was safe within the walls of the Jedi Temple, she no longer felt fully protected. As a youngling, she was brought there to learn the ways of the Force. The Temple had always been her center of peace, but now it was her source of dread. Darkness roamed its corridors and stalked her movements. Barriss had sensed its lurking existence ever since she returned.

Sharp panic rose in her chest. Memories of the battle on Geonosis still haunted her. Barriss tried to bury the anguish, but the visions rose up again. Lightsabers humming through the air as blaster bolts found their targets. Masters frantically seeking proof of life in motionless figures on the ground. The reverberating shouts and wails of agony mixed with the Separatists' clamoring glee and joy in death. These wraiths of memory filled her mind with torment.

Her master, Luminara Unduli, had protected them from the worst of the combat, and Barriss had fought bravely, a testament to her Padawan training. But the hordes of battle droids and Geonosian warriors had outnumbered them. Despite Master Yoda arriving with the clone troopers, so many of the Jedi had fallen.

She often wondered if a part of her had also perished in the bleak haze of the Petranaki Arena.

Barriss stood up from the meditation mat and adjusted her cloak with its fitted hood, smoothing over the blue patterned fabric. She slowly fingered the engraved heart on the buckle of her belt and took a series of deep breaths to calm the churning storm in her mind.

The traumatic loop of memories stopped, and the dark disturbance faded away, but Barriss knew they would both return.

When the Clone Wars began, Barriss did not go to the battlefront, despite being a highly trained and accomplished Padawan. She did not want to become a master of combat. The Force had always been a nurturing energy, and she did not believe it should be used for violence. Barriss did not want to fight.

So when her master became a general in the Grand Army of the Republic, Barriss remained at the Jedi Temple. She volunteered in the medical clinic and found solace helping injured Jedi. But it was very difficult to see so many of the Order harmed by the war, because their pain reflected her own. When they left her care and returned to their missions to fight the Separatists, Barriss knew far too well that their most catastrophic injuries could not be seen. The mental scars and emotional bruises brought a heavy burden. Through the Force, she sensed the turmoil of these Jedi returning into the theater of war, and their pain distressed her because she could not heal their deepest wounds.

Barriss now paced the small confines of her room. She could not bear to return to the medical clinic. Not after another failed meditation. She did not know if she could give encouragement or hope to those who needed it most. Not when war was waging across the galaxy and innocents were dying. The medical clinic had become a trigger for her own pain. Barriss could no longer heal others because she had not fully healed herself.

After another series of deep breaths, she reached out again into the Force. The darkness had not returned, and she embraced the soothing energy to quell her troubling thoughts. After her pulse returned to its normal rhythm, she left her room to walk the corridors of the Jedi Temple.

As a youngling, Barriss had marveled at the Great Hall, with its massive pillars and grand statues. With her clan of fellow Initiates, she had wandered through the high archways and manicured courtyards. In the evenings, Barriss had lingered on mezzanines to stare in awe at the Coruscant horizon filled with skyscrapers and endless streams of air traffic.

She continued her walk through the Temple and soon meandered onto a path that led to the youngling training levels. Entering one of the rooms, she stayed close to the back wall and observed a lesson.

Jedi Knight Tutso Mara moved along a line of young-lings as he instructed them in various lightsaber drills.

"Remember, the Force should guide your move-ments," the Jedi Knight said. "Let it lead you. Trust your instincts."

The training blades for the younglings did not have the same lethal energy as a Jedi lightsaber, allowing them to perform drills without fear of serious injury. Barriss still remembered the welts and bruises she had acquired while learning the Jedi forms with her own practice lightsaber.

She had not found joy in these lessons but in the Jedi Archives, where she would spend hours study-ing ancient texts. She had wanted to learn everything and yearned for the day when she would become a Padawan learner. Her deepest desire was to serve the galaxy as a member of the Jedi Order.

Barriss now sensed the flow of energy from the younglings as they embraced the Force. Tutso Mara walked among them and gently corrected their forms with reassurance. She felt a warmth of respect for him. Not so long before, she had been in this very room learning the fundamentals.

These younglings had only started their journey, not yet ready to travel to Ilum for the Gathering, where they would undergo the sacred rite of claiming kyber crystals and building their own lightsabers. Barriss stared at their eager young faces. They were so far removed from what was happening in the galaxy. War would not come to Coruscant. These younglings were far from harm and sheltered from the effects. But she still wondered if any of them sensed the dark disturbance that crept along the edges of her mind.

She knew the younglings were aware of the war. Many of their homeworlds were in its path, which placed their people in grave danger. The Jedi Council had made the decision to join the Republic's fight, and many innocents had become casualties in a war that seemed to have no end. These younglings would come of age in a galaxy filled with aggression and fear. Emotions that led to the dark side of the Force.

Barriss was now a Padawan. With more training, she would become a Jedi Knight. She wanted to serve not as a warrior but as a keeper of the peace. But the war had placed its brutal shadow over the future of the Jedi Order, and Barriss feared it would change everything.

The familiar sensation of doom spiked again in her chest. Barriss closed her eyes to practice her deep breathing. Slowly, she reached into the Force to ease the disquiet in her mind. When she was done, Tutso Mara was looking at her with deep concern. She knew he sensed her troubling thoughts. But then her wrist comlink lit up, and she heard Luminara Unduli's voice.

"Barriss, I need you to come to the Situation Room. There is an urgent matter we need to discuss."

"Yes, Master," she immediately responded.

Barriss bowed to Tutso Mara in a silent farewell and left the room to go meet her master.

Barriss arrived at the Jedi Situation Room and found her master speaking with Jedi Master Mace Windu. She stared at his hologram flickering above the strategy table. Barriss still remembered that fateful meeting in Chancellor Palpatine's office when Master Windu stated his concern about using the Jedi as soldiers. The Republic had been on the brink of war, and he had remained seated in deep contemplation when the other members of the Jedi Council had stood up to adjourn. The Chancellor had been firm that his negotiations would not fail, because the Republic had stood for a thousand years. But the Republic had fractured, and now Master Windu was a general waging war against the Separatists.

"It is imperative that you arrive at the Outer Rim Command Center to support the other generals,"

Master Windu said. "We will need reinforcements for the invasion."

Luminara Unduli motioned for Barriss to come forward and stand by her side. Master Windu acknowledged her presence with a solemn nod.

"I will notify Commander Gree to make ready," Master Unduli said. "My Padawan will be coming with me."

Barriss's stomach lurched at her master's words. She was going on a mission. Blinking away dark spots, she pressed her fingers over the engraved heart on her belt and maintained her composure.

"Very well. May the Force be with you." Master Windu bowed in farewell, and then his image disappeared.

Barriss straightened her posture when Luminara turned to her. The war had hardened the Jedi Master in many ways. Her green skin was paler than usual, making the black geometric markings on her chin more pronounced. Barriss was sure she displayed the same burden on her own face with the rite markings that spanned the bridge of her nose. But even with the weight of the war's effects, Luminara's strength and resolve glimmered in her deep blue eyes. The Mirialan Jedi was a highly respected member of the Order, and it was an honor for Barriss to be chosen as her Padawan.

"It is time for you to return to my side," Master Unduli said.

Barriss had known eventually she would have to join her master to fight in the war, and that time had finally come. She was grateful for the respite at the Jedi Temple, and although she had not fully healed from what she experienced on Geonosis, Barriss would have to be ready.

"I know this war has been hard on you, as it has been on all Jedi." Master Unduli's voice was softer. "But we have our duty, and we must serve."

"What is our mission?" Barriss asked, her voice steady.

Luminara closely examined Barriss for a moment before continuing. "The Jedi Council has learned the Geonosian archduke Poggle the Lesser has constructed several new weapons factories, so we will need to counter an invasion to retake Geonosis and destroy these factories once and for all."

The soothing energy Barriss had garnered from the Force left her body. Trickles of alarm traveled up her arms. She would have to return to Geonosis. The place where so many Jedi had fallen.

"We will be leaving soon to join the other Jedi," Master Unduli continued. "Kenobi and Skywalker perhaps have already formed a battle strategy, but I have been looking at other ways to destroy the threat, and I will need your help."

Luminara's face was stern, the valor in her eyes solid. She believed her Padawan was ready. There were no stirrings of doubt, or at least Barriss could not sense any.

"Yes, Master," Barriss quickly said. "Whatever needs to be done."

Luminara turned to the strategy table and pulled up a hologram of Geonosis. Zooming in on a collection of towering dirt spires, she focused on a schematic of vast catacombs that lay underneath one of the factory structures.

"If we can figure out a way to get to this main factory from underground, we can destroy it from within. This is what I need for you to determine."

Barriss moved closer to the hologram, staring at the numerous curves and turns of the Geonosian tunnels. She had already spotted a possible entry near one of the cliff walls. Barriss was so deep into her analysis, she hadn't heard her master's voice until Luminara called her name a second time.

"Barriss, this is very important. Will you be able to do this?"

"Yes, Master," she answered.

"You are more than capable, Padawan," Master Unduli stated. "I know I can depend on you. Skywalker will also have his Padawan with him. She can help once you gain entry inside the factory, so it will be up to you to guide her, as well."

Anakin Skywalker had been a Padawan himself during the first battle of Geonosis. Now he was a Jedi Knight. But unlike Barriss, his Padawan had left the safety of the Jedi Temple to fight by his side.

"Have you met her?" Barriss asked. "His Padawan?"

"Yes. Ahsoka Tano has inherited many of Skywalker's traits." A slight frown appeared on Luminara's face before it disappeared. "But she helped me fight a formidable Sith assassin, and for that I owe her my life."

Barriss felt a tug of guilt. She had not been by her master's side to protect her. She had been tucked away in the Jedi Temple, safe from the reality of war.

"I am grateful she was there for you, Master," Barriss said.

"We are finished with this briefing, and you have what you need." Master Unduli's voice was full of protocol and process again. "We will meet at the landing platform at oh six hundred hours. On our way to join Commander Gree and the Forty-First, you can update me on your progress. You may go now and prepare."

Barriss bowed in farewell and turned to leave, but then Luminara touched her arm and she promptly returned to her master's side.

"I trust you understand the importance of what I am asking you to do," Master Unduli said. "Your contribution could very well help end this war."

Barriss knew many innocents across the galaxy could be saved with the success of this mission. She did not want to fight, but she did want to serve.

"Yes, Master. I will do as you ask."

As the turbolift descended from the tower, Barriss tried to muster the courage to prepare for the mission.

She did not want to disappoint her master, but she felt the darkness emerging from its hiding place. It had sensed the fear and even perhaps the anger unfurling inside her. Barriss was returning to Geonosis, the place that had taken so many lives and produced so many scars.

But her master had not asked her to fight. Luminara had asked her to solve a problem.

Determining the best way to forge through the Geonosian tunnels was not a warrior task but an intellectual one. If she was successful in its completion, Barriss would play a pivotal role in restoring peace to the galaxy. She could help end the war. She could protect innocents from further suffering. She could start the process of healing herself.

Barriss was so deep in her thoughts that she did not see the Jedi Knight as he moved to her side. It wasn't until he spoke that she noticed him.

"It was very good to see you today, Barriss," Tutso

Mara said. "I still remember helping you properly hold a lightsaber."

Her face warmed at his presence. "My time as a youngling seems so far away, although it has not been that many years ago. I am sorry I had to leave your lesson before speaking with you. My master called for me."

"Master Unduli has returned to the Temple?"

"Yes," Barriss answered. "I am to go with her on a mission. We are helming an invasion on Geonosis."

Tutso raised his eyebrows at the news. Although he had left Coruscant many times for his own missions, he mostly remained at the Jedi Temple to help train the younglings.

"I sense your troubling thoughts about returning to the place that has caused you much distress," he said. "Do you feel you will be ready?"

Barriss released a long sigh, a surrender to her fate. "I do not have much choice in the matter."

Tutso nodded in agreement. "In these times, that is the case for most of us. The war has taken some of our choices away."

Barriss was not sure if he had any misgivings about the Jedi Council's decision to join the fight against the Separatists. But she highly respected him as a beloved friend and wanted to hear his opinion.

"Tutso, what are your feelings about this war? Do you feel the Jedi should be involved?"

"We are fighting on behalf of the Republic to restore peace to the galaxy," he answered.

"The Council has made us commanders and generals in the Republic Army. Is this the right way to be protectors of the peace?"

"Above all things, we must remember our duty as Jedi," Tutso said. "We cannot allow Count Dooku and the dark side of the Force to prevail."

Barriss remained quiet. She did not want to share her true feelings about the Jedi Council. Since the war began, Barriss had feared the Jedi were losing their way. But in many respects, Tutso was speaking the truth. If the Confederacy of Independent Systems won the war, it would only bring more turmoil and pain. Barriss had already sensed the dark side of the Force growing stronger. If the Republic failed, it would put the entire galaxy in danger.

They continued to walk in silence until Tutso asked her more details about her mission.

"Master Unduli wants me to study the catacombs beneath the surface of Geonosis. Our strategy is to find the best way to enter the main weapons factory so that we may destroy it." Barriss paused, unsure if she should share her struggles. "I know I can do what my master has asked of me, but . . . but I am finding it hard to focus."

"You cannot let your emotions deter you from your duty," Tutso reminded her.

"I am finding it very hard not to give in to my emotions. I know I must join the fight. . . ."

When Barriss trailed off, Tutso touched her

shoulder in reassurance. "It can be a difficult path. Do not give in to your fear. Trust in the Force."

"I will do my best," Barriss said.

He accompanied her to one of the courtyards. The air was warm, and Barriss closed her eyes to revel in the sunlight caressing her skin. She walked across the smooth stone to the Great Tree, with its massive trunk. Dark umber branches reached for the sky, and deep-gold leaves rustled in the breeze. As a Mirialan, Barriss had always been drawn to this natural entity. Like her people, she had a strong regard for and spiritual connection to plants and animals. In the courtyard of the Great Tree, she could not sense any darkness.

"I have not been able to meditate in my room," Barriss confessed. "But I find when I come here, it is possible."

The Jedi Knight moved forward and stood beside her. "It does not surprise me that you are drawn to this place. This uneti tree has a strong connection to the Force. It is why the Jedi Order brought it here."

Through the Force, she drew in calming energy and let it settle into her body. No darkness invaded her mind. No anger. No fear. Barriss sensed only peace and tranquility under the dappling shadows of the Great Tree. After a moment, Tutso took her hands in his.

"Let us meditate together here," he said.

Barriss returned to her room to prepare for her mission. Able to focus after meditating with Tutso Mara, she pulled up the hologram of the Geonosian catacombs and studied them until she had memorized every junction. She tentatively reached out into the Force, but the darkness still had not returned. Her mind remained clear and calm. Barriss delved deeper into her analysis, and soon she was able to determine the fastest route to the main factory.

Returning to Geonosis still stirred uneasy feelings. Like the other injured Jedi whom Barriss had treated in the medical clinic, her deepest wound had not healed. She did not know if full recovery was even possible. But she had done what had been asked of her, and Master Unduli would be very pleased. The accomplishment warmed her cheeks with pride.

Barriss would never be an eager commander in the Grand Army of the Republic, but her desire to serve and protect innocents was strong. If she could provide any assistance to end the death and suffering happening across the galaxy, then she would be fulfilling her duty. It was still a way to be a protector of the peace.

But doubt lingered inside of Barriss. If the war continued, would the Jedi be seen as protectors or warriors? The collateral damage of fighting the Separatists had been devastating so far. The loss of life in the Order was also a heavy burden. There were not many Jedi in the galaxy. But Barriss also knew the dark side of the Force was growing. The darkness was waiting for its chance to devour the Republic, and she feared that it could be already happening.

The first battle of Geonosis was the spark for the war, but maybe the second battle could be the solution to finally end it once and for all. Barriss planned to do her part to make sure the mission would be a success.

The landing platform was busy with activity, and Barriss walked among astromech droids and maintenance workers to meet her master as instructed. She remembered when she was a youngling and these hangars contained only transport ships and shuttles. Now they were filled with Jedi starfighters and gunships. It was another sobering effect of the war.

In addition to the fear, there was also a nip of bittersweetness. The Temple had been her home. She had learned the ways of the Force there and become a member of the Jedi Order. Now that she was leaving, she was not sure what kind of person she would be when she returned. Maybe when she met Anakin Skywalker's Padawan, Barriss could ask her how she coped with the fighting. Maybe Ahsoka Tano could reveal how she remained vigilant in the rules and regulations of the Jedi Order while also being a commander in a war.

She found her master in front of a clone transport ship with Commander Gree, prepping and organizing for deployment. Barriss would leave with them to join the clones of the 41st Elite Corps and then rendezvous with the rest of the assigned Republic fleet.

She bowed in acknowledgment when Luminara greeted her. "Master, I have done as you asked and completed the analysis of the Geonosian catacombs."

"Have you found a way for us to gain entry to the main factory?"

"Yes, Master," Barriss answered. "I have memorized all two hundred junctions, and I have also found the quickest way to enter the factory."

"I knew I could depend on you, my Padawan." Luminara gave her a small smile of satisfaction. "You will learn it is always best to be prepared."

A question formed on Barriss's tongue, but she hesitated to speak. Luminara sensed her discomfort and moved closer. "Barriss, do you wish to say something?"

"I do, Master. I have a question." She paused before speaking carefully. "Do you believe this invasion can end the war?"

Luminara pondered for a moment. "We cannot know what the future holds, nor the outcome of this mission. But I do know if we destroy Poggle's factories and retake Geonosis, we will be on the right path to end the war."

Barriss felt the truth in her master's words. The future could not be fully known. She sensed only the present moment in the swirl of activity of the landing platform. The darkness had receded, and she could no longer feel its presence. She was still afraid of the war, but she was not afraid to be a Jedi.

"I hope that will be the result, Master," Barriss said.

Luminara nodded in agreement and guided Barriss onto the clone transport ship. Her master examined her closely, and Barriss fidgeted under the focused gaze.

"Are you ready, Padawan?" Master Unduli finally asked.

A rumble of fear stirred in Barriss's chest and crawled up her throat, begging to be released in a scream. She wanted to reply with a thunderous refusal. But then she remembered Tutso Mara's words in the Temple courtyard, in front of the Great Tree.

Above all things, we must remember our duty as Jedi.

Barriss had done everything asked of her. She was prepared to return to Geonosis. She was prepared to do her duty. If she was successful, she could help the Republic end the war and return peace to the galaxy.

"Yes, Master," Barriss answered. "I am ready."

WORTHLESS

DELILAH S. DAWSON

AS ASAJJ VENTRESS tore through the heavy jungle, slashing vines with both lightsabers and leaping over fallen stone columns, she couldn't help thinking about how much easier this fight would be on a cold desert moon. But no, this abandoned palace complex was teeming with life, and most of those life-forms were just getting in her way.

Except for Obi-Wan Kenobi, who had thus far managed to stay one step ahead.

As soon as she'd spotted Kenobi, she'd left the Separatist droids behind and changed course to end her nemesis once and for all. He'd taken flight, but the terrain was no easier for him to navigate, with roots and vines slithering everywhere like snakes—and snakes, giant green things with fangs, slithering among them, too. At least the clones were performing just as poorly as their metallic counterparts in the droid army. It was a deadlock of the most infuriating kind.

Count Dooku had sternly commanded Ventress to take back the impenetrable ancient stronghold from the Republic. It was a place of strategic importance, he said, a grand sprawling complex surrounded by crumbling temples, aqueducts, and promenades, but the main palace appeared to lack any way inside. No doors, no windows, the stone too thick to carve open with a swipe of her blades. Peeking in through ornate fist-sized cutouts, she could see glimmers of columns and statuary within, but thus far, this battle seemed worthless.

Unless, of course, she was able to end the wily Jedi

who had already evaded her too many times to count.

And then she would inform Count Dooku of her success.

Kenobi bounded ahead of her, and she followed down the crumbling promenade, speeding up, lengthening her stride, lightsabers twirling in her hands. She'd been dreaming of this moment, of what she would do when the Jedi finally lay on the ground at her feet with no one to save him, nowhere left to run, and nothing left to do but beg for his pathetic life.

She was almost within striking distance. So close. He was flagging, too, sweat darkening his hair and leaving stains on the back of his robes. Kenobi leapt over a fallen stone column and turned to face her, lightsaber in hand, his face a mask of concentration. Ventress leapt, lightsabers swinging down for the killing stroke, and—

Crack!

She felt the impact before she understood what was happening. A huge chunk of stone slammed into her body, one of the columns pulled down on her back by that rancid slime Kenobi. The lightsabers flew out of her fingers as she prepared to use the Force to repel the falling stone before it could crush her. She twisted in the air, hands up, and her back landed on the mass of vines, and—

She was falling into nothingness—into some sort of giant pit.

The ground had disappeared, and Ventress, for once, was caught by surprise. There was nothing to push against, just empty space. She flailed in midair like a panicked tooka cat, struggling to understand which way was up, which way was down, and which way would lead her back to her clever prey on the planet's surface.

Whoomp.

A piece of old masonry, jutting out into the empty

space, exploded against her left leg. Pain shot through her body, red lightning bolts of heat and a dull numbness that she knew wasn't good.

Things were happening so fast that she couldn't keep up. Pain blurred her senses. Vines pressed into her stomach and then snapped, carved buttresses crumbled with her impact, and still the heavy stone column pressed her down as she plummeted toward what she assumed would be a very hard floor. She could only watch helplessly as she tumbled past elaborate catwalks and balconies, just as old and beautiful as the ones around the palace, built into the huge pit.

Smack.

Something slammed against the back of her head, and her vision went black and then sparkled with stars. When she opened her eyes, she was forced to look down and face the inevitable, her head reeling with dizziness. She usually felt lithe and powerful, unstoppable, but it was as if her body was moving through mud, her fractured brain not quite connected to her pain-addled limbs.

Ventress crashed face-first into a massive carpet of vines. Before she could thank the gods for the cushioned landing, the falling stone hit the ground and broke in half, trapping her lower legs. For a long moment, she lay there, feeling every ache in her body and hoping beyond hope that nothing was badly damaged. But the moment she twisted to sit up, she knew the truth.

Broken.

Her stupid, traitorous leg was broken.

Groaning, she struggled onto her elbows to take in her surroundings.

The pit was enormous: perfectly round, clearly architectural and in no way natural. The bridges, balconies, and catwalks she'd slammed into on her way down made exquisite patterns, seen from below. If she'd had her full powers and use of all her limbs, she could've climbed out easily.

But there she was, exhausted and broken, nause-atingly dizzy, riddled with pain—and missing her weapons.

And Kenobi was probably up there at the very top, laughing at her, so far away that she could see only a white-hot circle of light.

The trapdoor overhead slowly groaned as it eased back into place, and then the pit was completely dark and utterly silent.

She whipped out her comlink. "Ventress calling for immediate extraction."

There was no answer.

There was no signal.

She was trapped and alone.

And yet . . . perhaps not entirely alone.

"Who's there?" Ventress barked, reaching out through the Force. Thanks to the throbbing in her head and the pain in her leg, her connection to the Force was horrifically, embarrassingly weak—and dis-tracted by the annoying amount of life that flourished on this planet. Every surface was covered in vines. In every crevice, lizards and insects and snakes and some kind of scraggle-toothed half bird, half rodent lived their small lives. And over there, somewhere, holding very, very still—a person.

"I know you're there," she said with a scowl. "Don't make me come kill you to find out who exactly you are."

She wasn't sure she *could* kill anyone in her current state, but they didn't know that.

The form stood, wary, its hand going for a holster.

"Don't bother trying to kill me, clone," she hissed. "It's a waste of everyone's time."

"Bold words for someone who can't stand up," the man observed with that same voice, same accent of every clone she'd ever encountered. He was brave, speaking to her like that—or foolhardy.

And, much to her frustration, he was also correct.

"I won't always be wounded," she reminded him.

"But you are now."

Ventress sighed through clenched teeth, hating the truth of it. The clone didn't come closer, so she took a quick inventory. Her leg and head were the real problems; everything else ranged from slightly bruised to perfectly fine, but her leg was badly broken and she was fairly certain she had a concussion. Throwing all her concentration into the gesture, she attempted to use the Force to push herself up off the ground and free herself from the column, but it was no use. Thanks to the concussion, her usual powers were flickering like a fried droid. The cracked stone barely twitched.

"Clone!" she barked. "If you want to live, help me with this blasted hunk of rock."

The clone didn't move. "Seems like you're probably safer where you are, if you can't move it yourself."

She snarled a sigh. "Leave it to a clone to be so infuriatingly logical and uncreative."

Robbed of her powers and weapons, she was

as helpless as she'd ever been, but she still had her cunning—something, she well knew, clones were bred specifically not to possess.

"Let me guess," she drawled, "you fell through the trapdoor, and you've been down here long enough to know there's no exit. You've tried climbing up and failed. You're starting to feel hopeless."

"Trapped down here with a Sith, who wouldn't feel hopeless?" he shot back.

An excellent point.

"Ah, but if we agree to work together, perhaps we can both live to fight another day."

A pause as he considered it. "How do I know you won't betray me? Isn't that what your kind is known for?"

"I have no kind. I am no Sith."

A pause as he reset. "Then what are you?"

"Angry. Merciless. And burdened with a long memory for those who've failed me."

She twitched her leg experimentally where it lay under the stone and felt the bones scrape together.

Yes, he was her only option.

"I can't escape without you, and you can't escape without me. I suggest a truce."

"And if you turn on me?" he asked.

"I might ask the same question."

The vines crunched as he navigated toward her. He had a small lantern that lit the chamber with glowing bluish light. Ventress had to shield her eyes and look away from the brightness.

"What do you swear by?" he asked. "What do you hold sacred?"

"These days, nothing," she admitted.

"What about this?"

Bright red light seared the darkness as one of her lightsabers burned to life, illuminating the familiar dull face of a clone. Fear bloomed in her heart, and she looked away, her tender skull shuddering in agony at the brightness. Right now, at this very moment, she could be easily slain by this unworthy maggot, and there was nothing she could do about it.

"That, I'll swear by." She held out her hand for the saber, her palm itching to hold it.

"I think I'll keep it," he warned. "Just to make sure you keep your part of the bargain."

"You understand that once I have my full capabilities, I'll take it back and kill you with it?"

The words had less bite when said while lying on the ground, splayed out like a bug.

He tipped the blade toward her face, and she flinched from the heat.

"I'm sure you will. Now how do we get out?"

Ventress sighed. This was going to be . . . uncomfortable.

"We must get the stone off my leg. Clone, you'll have to help. My powers are . . . not at their zenith."

The red light disappeared, and she heard her saber slide into his blaster holster. She briefly bared her teeth in rage at the sound of the sacred object rattling against his pathetic armor. He held his lantern over her leg, gave the stone an experimental shove.

"My name's not Clone. They call me Doc."

"Are you a medic?"

"No. It's a nickname. Now, listen. If I use both hands and you use whatever powers you can muster, we should be able to get it off."

" 'Should,' " she muttered. "A stupid word."

The clone—Doc—hooked his lantern onto his uniform and put both hands to the stone. "Ready? On three. One, two . . ."

When he said "three," Ventress closed her eyes and connected with the Force, but what would've normally been a mighty heave that sent the stone smashing into the wall was barely a shove. Combined with the clone's push, however, it was just enough. With one annoying wobble, the bit of architecture toppled off her legs, and she rolled free with a groan.

"Anything broken?" the clone asked.

"Nothing a little bacta won't cure," she said with more bravado than she felt.

He placed the lantern on the vines, and when Ventress felt the clone's gloved hands on her leg, her temper flared like a supernova. Under any other circumstances, she would've incinerated him on the spot, but—

"Compound fracture," he stated simply. "If I can find a stick, I'll splint it, use the little vines as rope."

"Do, then," she commanded.

He gave her a brief annoyed glare. "You're not my boss."

"You're a clone. Everyone is your boss. That's the point of your existence."

His only response was a tired sigh.

As he hunted around with his lantern, she managed to sit up, although it made her dizzy. Much to her surprise, the clone soon had her leg neatly splinted and helped her stand with minimal discussion. She'd thought to slip her lightsaber from his holster, but he'd done something else with it while he worked on her leg. He was smarter than he looked.

"Better?" he asked.

"Functional," she responded blandly, testing it and nearly falling over, thanks to the uneven ground. It was, she hated to admit, a job well done. "Now, help me to the wall."

Once Ventress had her hand against the wall, she swallowed down her nausea—this dratted concussion!—and the strangest thing happened. She felt the Force flowing through the ancient stone with unusual power, unlike anything she'd ever experienced. The piece of architecture that had fallen on her was a normal material, but this odd pink stuff—the same used for the bastion overhead—was something very, very different. It met her with the joy of a long-neglected Corellian hound, calling forth visions more vivid than life. Long ago, this pit had been grand, the walls beautifully carved and painted, free from vines. Jedi of a strange, small, slender species had somersaulted and leapt from the courtyard overhead down to the bridges and buttresses, landing on the floor of the pit in their billowing robes, where they moved in a processional to—

Ventress hobbled along the wall and pressed a design carved in the stone that anyone else might've overlooked. With a complaining grumble, a painfully narrow door slid open, revealing an even more impenetrable darkness beyond.

"Clever," Doc noted.

"But not safe. And a tight fit, even for me." She looked at him by the light of his lantern. The lightsaber was back in his holster—both of them were, actually. "You'll have to take off your armor, I think."

Doc shook his head. "No way. And be even more vulnerable in a tight space with you?"

Ventress rolled her eyes—and instantly regretted it

when her head pulsed with pain. "We're both vulnerable down here. You'll just have to trust me."

He threw up his hands. "People who trust you die!"

"Then I guess you'll have to choose whether you'd rather die here, now, or in three days from dehydration at the bottom of this pit."

The clone put a hand on his holster. "How do I know you're not using mind tricks on me?"

Ventress snorted. "Because you would need a mind to control, and we both know you're a clone, which means you have no mind of your own. Separated from your compatriots and leaders, you're worthless."

"Worth enough to get you out from under that rock."

She chuckled. "I suppose that's fair. Now take off the armor, and let's get moving."

Before I pass out, she didn't say. Her head was pounding like a drum, her leg a white-hot bolt of lightning. She wouldn't let the clone know that, though.

Doc stripped off his armor, leaving a black bodysuit. She hadn't seen his helmet, but he pulled a piece of fabric from somewhere, unfolded it to make a bag, and shoved all the plates and her sabers into it.

"After you," he said.

Turning sideways, Ventress slipped into the cramped hallway. With her hand against the eager stone, her Force sensing came in bursts, the stone's visions alerting her to several cunning traps. First came a swiping blade from overhead; she paused to let it pass, then moved beyond it. "Now," she told the clone, and he moved quickly to follow her past the first trap. This test had been designed for the planet's Jedi, who'd apparently had an affinity for this particular oddly responsive stone. An unusual specialty, but perhaps that was why they'd died out, leaving this once-grand palace empty—perhaps their powers weren't so useful against beings who could fight back.

The next obstacle was a pressure-sensitive trap-door, and Ventress stepped over it and helped Doc across. He had to turn sideways, stomach sucked in, body contorted just to fit. His bag of armor rattled along with him, worsening her headache—and making her want to inflict similar harm.

"I suppose it's good that you were bred to follow orders," she noted. "You're doing an admirable job of doing exactly as I tell you."

"Was that a compliment or a dig?" Doc said.

"Can it not be both? I simply have doubts about anyone who follows orders without question."

"You follow orders, too," Doc reminded her. "And I've questioned you multiple times."

"Yet here we are."

"Here we *both* are. If my choices are to die in a pit or take a chance that there's some sliver of good left in you, I suppose optimism won out. And I'm still alive, so it seems like the right choice."

She held up a hand to halt him as slender metal lances shot across the narrow space, then slowly withdrew. After they'd both moved beyond the trap, she said, "Or perhaps you've been programmed to tell yourself it's the right choice."

He grunted as he navigated a particularly narrow passageway. "Even if my origins aren't ideal, at least I know that I'm on the right side of the fight."

"The right side is the side that wins," Ventress hissed.

"Clever words, but you're not on the ground, watching a planet's people lose their way of life, their village and family and friends, simply because Dooku decided a place is valuable. The Separatists just want to rule. They don't want to help. They don't care about freedom."

"Funny, that you have no freedom, yet you fight for the freedom of strangers."

The clone shrugged as much as the space would allow. "I guess that's what sacrifice is, isn't it? Giving up something valuable in the hopes that others can have something even better."

"I'd call that stupidity."

"Maybe that's why you're alone."

When she tried to whirl around to punish him for such insolence—she couldn't. The hallway was so narrow that she could only sidle through it. "You'll pay for that," she promised him.

"It only hurts because it's true."

Ventress was so angry she almost missed the next trap, barely jerking back before a stone block slammed down where she'd been standing. "Silence," she barked, wincing at the noise she'd just made. "If you make me miss something, we both die."

Doc did indeed go quiet, but there was an unspoken sense that he'd won, which made Ventress all the more determined to escape and kill him. She could've easily let him fall to one of the traps, but then . . . what if they reached the next test and she needed his strength, strength her injuries denied her?

Fine. For now, she would let him think he'd won.

He was nothing. It was like letting a gundark believe it had triumphed.

Ventress could sense that they were almost through the claustrophobic tunnel, and with just a few more pauses, she emerged in a more open space. It wasn't large by any means, but at least she could take a full breath. She limped aside, making room for Doc. He stepped out into the open hall and took a great gasp of air.

"That was a tight fit," he observed as he put his armor back on with practiced quickness and slid her sabers into his holster.

Her fingers itched for them, but . . . did she even have the strength to lift them?

Later. She'd take them back later and make him pay.

"Of course it was tight. We're lucky the locals weren't even smaller. Now hush. Let me figure out this new place." When she put her hand on the wall, it was just as much to steady herself as it was to get a sense of their next challenge. She had the strongest urge to sleep, to curl up against the wall and take a nap. And that alone told her what bad shape she was in—that her fractured mind could even consider going unconscious with an armed clone nearby and no protection.

She had to fight it.

She had to get out of there.

Her connection with the Force felt like frayed wires spitting sparks, but the stone was more than willing to pour visions into her mind like a fountain gushing into cupped hands. It told her that this new place was a maze. It wasn't broken up into rooms and hallways but was rather a series of nonsensical stops and starts and dead ends. The ceiling overhead and the floor below were solid, meters and meters of stone. And the walls of the maze were too thick for her to carve her way through with her lightsabers, even if she'd had them both in hand.

"It's a maze," she told Doc. "With no clear path."

"Can't you, I don't know—just see it? With your powers?" he asked stupidly.

"Yes, of course, why didn't I think of that?" she spat. "Oh, wait. It must be *this life-threatening brain injury!*" With her hand on the wall, visions of wandering Jedi pulsed through her head like a garbled transmission, but the stone didn't have any concept of route, only of history. Useless.

"I heard General Kenobi talk about a maze once," Doc said. "Something from an old myth. He said that if you're ever lost, you should put your hand on the wall and keep walking to the right, always making right turns, and it will eventually lead you out."

"That's a stupid thing to do," Ventress growled, closing her eyes as she sought the secret to escape and found nothing but pain and annoying flashes of tranquil Jedi.

"Well, the general's not currently trapped in a maze, so it must've worked for him at least once.

Might as well try it. Unless you want to just stand there frowning." He put his hand on the wall to their right and began walking, the way ahead lit only by his lantern. He turned back. "Are you able to sense any traps?"

"No." She took her hand off the wall and limped after him. "This place is its own trap. If you can't find your way out, you starve to death."

She could tell Doc had slowed his pace to accommodate her, and she hated him for it. She wanted out, now, fast, but instead they were slowly tracing the walls of the stupid ancient maze. The stone's visions had revealed it was once part of a ritual, but she felt nothing holy there. Without its people and their dedication, it was an empty, dead space. Perhaps a battle raged overhead, but down there, all was silent. Funny, that this place was the entire reason they were fighting. There were artifacts in the fortress, Dooku had said. Possibly holocrons or other useful objects. So far, she'd seen nothing but talkative stone and threats.

She'd like to throw Dooku down there and see what sort of a strategic advantage it gave him.

As she followed the clone, hating him, hating everything, she longed for an honest contest. For an enemy to fight—preferably that grotesque little imp, Kenobi—or a beast to vanquish or a ship to race. Here was a situation she couldn't dominate using the Force or her fighting skills or even cunning. Her brain and her powers were hobbled, and all she could do was follow, of all things, a clone—a useless waste of air. She couldn't fight her way out or think her way out; the only way through was stubbornly taking step after step, even when she wanted to stop and nap. She followed the little lantern, her fingertips tracing dully over ancient stone, the first living person to breathe this air in millennia. She was sustained only by her rage, by thoughts of what she would do to Kenobi when she escaped.

Their path led into dead ends, through curving hallways, and up and down stairs, which took her a maddening amount of patience to navigate. Doc tried to help her once, and she clawed at him like a furious beast. He didn't try again. Halfway up a stairwell, she turned and sank to sitting, her bad leg held out stiffly at an uncomfortable angle. Twisting in place, she laid her forearms along a step, her cheek upon her shoulder.

"Ventress?" Doc called.

"Leave me be."

She could feel his regard as he looked down at her. His pity. "We need to keep going," he finally said.

"Then keep going. I just need a little rest, and then I'll be able to find my own way. I don't need you. I don't need anyone."

He shuffled his boots a bit. He was tempted to go, she could tell. If he could get out alive, he could tell Kenobi exactly where to find her—injured and without her greatest weapons. In this state, there was no way she could best the Jedi. He would carve her down like a nerf steak. But—well, the clone would surely die on his way out. There would be other tests, other challenges he couldn't escape alone, not without her Force-enhanced senses and cunning. It was a curious partnership indeed, and had their situations been reversed, she would've put him out of his misery and gotten out all the quicker without an injured clone dragging her down.

"You shouldn't sleep with a concussion," he warned, sitting on a step beside her. "You might never wake up."

"What do you know?"

"I'm not a medic, but they call me Doc for a reason. I have an instinct. About medicine, bodies. You need to keep moving."

"So let me stop and die. Wouldn't that be best for the Republic?"

A sad chuckle. "Perhaps, but not best for my conscience. Come on. Let's get outside. Then we can try to kill each other like civilized people."

The absolute nerve of the man, to grab her under

her arm and yank her up! She tried to swat him away, but he was strong, and every movement hurt her. She let him drag her to standing, let him sling her arm around his neck. He mostly carried her up those last few stairs, and she didn't complain, she didn't curse him. She just tried to stay awake and keep going, the animal deep in her heart desperate to see the sun again, no matter the cost.

Together, him doing most of the work, they hobbled up the stairs and kept following that wall wherever it led. It took such effort to stay awake when she wanted so badly to taste the sweet oblivion of sleep.

As she limped down the hall, hating the stench of his sweat, she realized that something had changed. There was light—just a little bit, just enough to show the faded chalky paintings on the walls. This was a warm light, so different from his lantern.

"I think we're almost out," Doc said.

The hallway terminated in a large room lit by arrows of sunlight shining in through the ornate flower-shaped holes she'd noticed from outside the massive stone walls. It was clever, how the small dots brightened the hall but kept it dry and safe. Upon further inspection, she realized this grand chamber was some kind of museum. Carved pedestals placed at regular intervals held the ancient artifacts Dooku had promised she would find, if she could fight her way into the fortress. She could see at least one holocron, several statuettes, pieces of jewelry, a very rustic lightsaber hilt carved from some kind of animal tooth.

Ventress snapped awake in that moment.

First, because she knew that this room was the entire reason she and her army were there in the first place.

And second, because she didn't have to touch the telling stone to know it was a trap.

But Doc didn't know, apparently. The absolute fool reached for the rustic lightsaber hilt.

"Hey, that looks like a—"

Ventress's hands flew up, and she reached deep into

her soul and channeled every bit of power she could find as she threw Doc across the room.

Or tried to.

If she'd been at full strength, he would've slammed into the far wall, possibly breaking it—and definitely breaking most of his bones. As it was, she knocked him aside before he could touch the treasure. He didn't fly so much as he fell over, but he was on the ground, either way.

And she was drained to nearly nothing, barely catching herself on the wall.

"What was that for?" Doc asked, sounding angry and hurt.

"It's a trap," she managed to say between big gulps of air. "Touch nothing."

Doc stood and considered the lightsaber hilt. It didn't look like a trap, but then again, traps rarely did. That was why they were both down there in the first place.

"Thanks for that," he said.

She flicked her fingers at him, hating that her instincts were so soft. "Just help me over to that door."

Across the hall, there was indeed the outline of a grand doorway, although she recalled no matching markings outside. That same strange pink stone from down below dominated the chamber, giving it a holy, regal glow. Doc again slung her arm over his shoulder as if she wasn't a perfect killing machine and slowly helped her hop across the room past artifacts so important that war was being waged for them outside, his brothers dying just meters away, their blood soaking into the dirt for objects they couldn't use, much less appreciate. At the door, she put her palm to the eager pink stone that flowed so rich with the Force, and was gifted with a brief vision of a sad old being opening this door for the last time, tears dripping from wide round eyes.

She touched the correct carving, and the door shuddered up, revealing light so bright she had to shield her eyes. As soon as it began to open, they heard the fighting beyond. The zap of blasters, the call of orders, the perky chirp of "Roger, roger."

"Are you going to kill me now?" Doc asked, eyes flicking to the arm around his neck.

Ventress pulled her arm away, rubbed it like it had some sort of stink on it. Without meeting his eyes, she snatched her lightsabers from his holster. She held them up, facing him, knowing full well that if she pushed the buttons, he'd be dead with practically no work on her part.

But she didn't push those buttons.

"What's the point?" she said blandly. "I told you— you're worthless. Just one of many, bred to die."

With a nod, she hobbled over to a balustrade and sat. Ignoring him completely, she pulled out her comlink.

"I've infiltrated the fortress. You have my coordinates," she said. "Bring a battalion to take control. And bring me a med droid."

When she looked up, Doc was gone.

Maybe he wasn't as foolish as she'd assumed.

Shielding her eyes, she stared out at the raging battle, hunting for the familiar brown-clad form of Kenobi, but all she saw were droids and clones, seemingly infinite re-creations of the same two forms, a writhing pit of useless killing.

She closed her aching eyes. Kenobi could wait another day.

Alone again, alone always, she waited for the droids to obey her command.

THE GHOSTS OF MAUL

MICHAEL MORECI

AT LAST, *we will have revenge.*

Such naïve words spoken by such a naïve person. What did I know when I said that to my former master, Darth Sidious? Nothing. I knew *nothing.*

But since then, I've learned.

Reconstructing myself on Lotho Minor, I learned.

Being healed by my mother and the Nightsisters, I learned.

Wielding the power of the Darksaber, I learned.

Now Darth Sidious—or Emperor Palpatine; whatever name he wishes to call himself means little to me—is the one whose mind is in the dark. Looking out onto the Coruscant skyline, he and I, master and apprentice, spoke of revenge as if he knew something about it. As if he knew what it is like to be discarded and forgotten, to be broken and mangled. He is the one who knows *nothing* of these things. None of them do. Not Sidious, not Kenobi.

But I do. I know what it's like to have the fire of vengeance burning deep within you, to understand that the things that have been taken from you can never be returned. The only path to satisfying your fury is balancing the scales; you must take from others what has been taken from *you*.

Which is why I'm here, on this gloomy, ashen gray planet. I can feel the grit of the arid ground with every step I take, passing between trees so dry and so brittle that I wonder how they manage to stand. Their bare, crooked branches twist upward, jabbing into the sky as if they're pleading for someone above to rescue them. Though the feeling is faint, I can sense through the

Force that something terrible happened here; a dark power once passed through every living thing, poisoning and overwhelming it, leaving it as I see it now.

Dead. Desolate.

It brings a smile to my face.

Damanos is what they once called this planet. Lost to most star charts, I tracked down its precise location through no small amount of will and, when the situation called for it, aggressive displays of power. It was no simple task to find a planet that most assume exists only in myth, but if the prize in my sights is indeed real, it will have been worth the effort.

Ahead, the jagged trees begin to thin, clearing the view to the world ahead. My pace quickens as I feel something pulling me forward—something hungry for fear and anger.

I know I must be getting close.

My hand instinctively reaches for the lightsaber at my side. Though alone, I still feel danger in this place; it permeates from everywhere, a subtle yet clear warning that darkness abounds, and all who dare approach it do so at their own risk.

Understanding that doesn't make me turn away; it makes me approach even faster.

At last, I come to a rise overlooking a fathomless ravine below. But most important, beyond the obsidian crevice stands what I came to find—

The castle.

But not just any castle, no.

A Sith castle.

Constructed of stone as black as Damanos itself, its towers and keep reach high enough to pierce the low-hanging clouds, leaving anyone to wonder just how high they ascend. Vines once attempted to scale its sides but failed, leaving behind nothing but their own decay. Walls seem to stand and meet in predictable fashion, but there is also something unusual about their union. Every angle, every corner—it all appears to be chaos. The castle seems impossible, yet somehow inevitable at the same time. And the more I look at it, the more physically unsettled I become.

Luckily, I didn't come all this way simply to take in the view. My destination is inside the castle and the Sith secrets—secrets that will grant me knowledge and, most important, *power*—that I am certain lie within.

There's no time to spare.

The front doors push open with a creak. Inside, the castle is all but empty—save for the secrets that will finally give me the power to locate and destroy my enemies. It is the Sith way, after all, to hoard dangerous knowledge and never share it with others, even those closest to you. *Especially* those closest to you.

Moldering statues of cloaked figures line the walls, and as I pass them, one by one, it's almost as if I can feel their eyes following me. Not to look at me, but to look *into* me. They were no doubt Lords of the distant and forgotten past, or at least so say the legends that stand in the place of any real history this castle—even this entire planet—will ever offer. And yet I can still feel it, radiating from every meter of this place—the power of the dark side.

I know I am not alone.

"*Maul.*"

A voice calls for me from the shadows overhead. I turn toward a wide, winding staircase that leads to the next floor, and the voice—a deep growling whisper—calls again.

"*Maul.*"

I'm halfway up the staircase when I hear an all-too-familiar sound; it's the crackle and humming energy of a lightsaber.

A red, double-bladed weapon emerges from the utter blackness at the top of the staircase. Savage Opress, my brother, is gripping the hilt.

My *dead* brother.

"Brother," I say. I take my own lightsaber into my grasp, though I don't ignite it—not yet.

"I am no brother of yours," Savage says, and though his voice comes from his mouth, I do more than hear it. I can feel it flowing through me, like the dark side of the Force itself.

"No brother of mine?" I respond. "I see. Is that because you are not truly who you appear to be, or because you believe there's some sort of justice in severing our family bond?"

"You failed me, Maul. You were my master and my brother, and you failed at both. I wasn't like you, but you tried to mold me into your image nonetheless. All to serve your thirst for *revenge*."

I reach the top of the stairs, within striking distance of the man who was once my only ally in the entire galaxy.

"I never wanted you to fall," I say. "I only wished for you to have power. For both of us to have power and stand side by side in a world that feared us."

Savage sneers and pulls back his lightsaber. I know what's going to happen next. "And look where we both ended up."

I ignite my lightsaber, deflecting Savage's powerful strike just as his blade flashes toward my face.

"Why are you here?" Savage asks as his lightsaber presses against mine. He's strong, and the force of his strength, fueled by his rage, sends me back on my heels. "What can you possibly need in a lost domain of the Sith?"

I twist away from Savage and swing my blade at his feet; he leaps, dodging the attack, and I take a step back so we have some separation.

"You know what I want," I say as Savage and I circle each other, each waiting for the other to strike. "I want nothing more than to balance the scales, for what they did to you, to our mother, and to me."

Savage begins to laugh, mocking me. "You don't want revenge. Maybe once, long ago, that is what drove you. But now . . . now you fear. I can feel it in you. What you truly want, *Darth Maul*, is to not feel powerless."

The rage swells in me with every word he says. By the time he finishes, I'm on top of him, crashing my lightsaber into his. Through the crimson light burning from where our blades meet, I can see him straining to hold me back.

"The Sith took everything from me! Including you, my brother. It seems only right that I turn their own power against them and use it to watch them burn. To watch *everything* burn!"

I pull my weapon away from his and bring it down again. Savage brings his blade up just in time to parry, and I see the fear in his eyes. His posture is defensive; it's timid and weak. I would be ashamed for my brother if I didn't realize the truth—

This dark sorcery, whatever it is, has not brought back Savage Opress.

This is nothing more than an *imposter*.

Our lightsabers clash again, and I spin my bottom

blade upward. The move catches Savage by surprise, and it forces his weapon out of his grip. I hear the lightsaber clatter to the ground, lost in the darkness below.

He tries to back away, but there's nowhere for him to go. I have him cornered. I grab him by the back of his neck and pull him toward me, so this apparition and I can look each other in the eye. That's when he starts to beg.

Pathetic.

"Brother, stop. I died once already because of you. Don't—"

"You," I say, my teeth bared, "are no brother of mine."

I push my blade through this imposter's belly, and he crumples lifelessly to the ground. I draw my lightsaber back and nudge the body lying at my feet out of the way.

For just a moment I look down, though I don't know why. He's just another fallen enemy, after all, another obstacle removed from my path. Perhaps I need to be certain that he's gone, or perhaps I simply wish to see the face of my brother one last time.

Any hopes for such a parting glance evaporate the moment I cast my eyes downward. Savage has somehow changed; I'm not looking at the face of my brother—

I'm looking at my own.

Then I hear a voice, whispering across the cavernous space—Savage's voice.

"You. Failed. Me," it says.

I look back at my own self one last time. My lifeless eyes stare back at me. I growl, turn off my lightsaber, and continue on my way.

Deeper inside the castle, I enter what appears to be the throne room. Every step I take resounds across this massive space, and I can't help wondering the last time anyone—anyone of living flesh and blood—walked these floors.

Paintings, fading and obscured with dust, hang from the walls. They depict various battle scenes, each more gruesome than the last. In every image, a small group of figures, armored and cloaked so their faces cannot be seen, fight off waves of invading forces. They all possess lightsabers—the cloaked figures, that is—their blades the customary Sith crimson. I can only imagine what life was like on the planet, and in this castle, however many generations ago.

Unforgiving, it would seem. If there's one thing I know about the Sith, it's that they are, and always will be, defined by their treachery—a trait that is equaled only by the hypocrisy of their Jedi enemies.

As I pass through this room, I sense a great energy coming from deeper within the castle. Though all life on this planet may be extinguished, the power of the dark side is still strong. It's leading me somewhere, but where—and for what purpose—I know not.

Just as I'm about to reach the doors to the next room, a sound catches my attention. It's like the patter of feet hurrying across the floor, but they move too quickly to belong to any human.

I turn, hearing the sound again, and I move just in time to see a shape crawling across the room. It disappears into the darkness before I recognize it. Whatever it is, I know it is no ally.

I ignite my double-bladed lightsaber, and the blades sizzle through the darkness.

"Reveal yourself!" I yell, and my voice echoes back at me.

The skittering scratches the floor behind me once again. I turn quickly but see nothing but a figure maneuvering through the shadows.

"Do you think you frighten me?" I say. "Whatever you are, you're nothing but an echo of your former power. Reveal yourself, and let me show you what I mean."

Then I hear it once more, the sound of movement over my shoulder. But the figure is not moving across—oh, no, no. It's moving *up*, and I know exactly who I'm destined to find the moment I turn around.

"Greetings, Darth Maul," says the raspy voice. I look up and find General Grievous pouncing from the ceiling, his four lightsabers bearing down on me. "I've been expecting you."

I roll out of Grievous's path, and his blades slice the air where I once stood, narrowly missing me. When I get back to my feet, I grip my lightsaber tight, narrow my eyes, and glare at the enemy before me.

"You," I say through my clenched teeth.

"It's been so long since we last met on Dathomir," Grievous responds.

I don't say anything as we circle each other. It seems like the room has grown darker. Grievous is barely visible, even with his four lightsabers—two blue, two green—giving light to the space around him.

"You must remember when you last saw me," Grievous continues, then pauses to violently cough. "You watched as I killed your precious Mother Talzin."

"Yes," I say, keeping my eyes on the cyborg. "And then Kenobi killed *you*."

Grievous hacks out a maniacal laugh. It echoes across the entire room. "And how did that make you feel? Knowing that your sworn enemy stole your revenge from you?"

Fury ignites within me. Fury, and then hatred. There's another feeling there, deep within me, but I ignore it and focus on my rage instead. It gives me strength; it gives me *power*.

I scream and lunge at Grievous, slashing my lightsaber against his. I quickly relieve him of one of his lightsabers, and he bellows out in pain. I strike at him again and again, unleashing my anger; my crimson blades move in aggressive arcs, and soon I've taken away another one of Grievous's lightsabers—and the appendage attached to it.

And yet, despite being pinned down, he laughs.

"I remember your face when I killed your mother," Grievous says. "So much anguish. I wonder if you'll make the same face as I drive my lightsabers into you next."

"You are not real!" I yell in his face.

"No, I'm not. But tell me—knowing that the person who took your mother from you is dead, did it bring you any comfort? Did you find peace in my demise?"

I don't know what to say. My breathing is so labored it sounds like a growl, and that's the only sound I manage to make.

"I didn't think so," Grievous says, answering for me. One of his mechanical legs kicks out, catching me off guard. It drives into my chest and knocks me back.

I immediately get into a defensive position, expecting Grievous to attack. But he doesn't. He simply stands there, not saying a word. My anger still burns within me; I could not control it if I wanted to.

"I never asked for any of this!" I bark at the monstrous cyborg before me. "You and your masters took everything from me! My family, my power—you left me with nothing!"

"You didn't ask for this, that much is true," Grievous says, "but you never leave it behind."

I roar as I rush Grievous again, spinning forward and swinging my blades against his. No matter how powerfully I attack, no matter how much I use my hatred, he defends strike after strike. And oddly, he never goes on the offensive.

"What do you feel, Maul?" Grievous asks, taunting me. "When you think about Mother Talzin? About Savage? When you think about how quickly Sidious abandoned you when you fell?"

"Anger! And it is the weapon I'll use to destroy you—all of you!"

Our weapons clash, and I twist around, slicing another hand and leaving him with only one final saber. Grievous is somehow unaffected by his injuries.

"What else?" he asks, pressing me, toying with me. "There's more; we both know it."

"There is nothing but my rage!"

I feel like an open wound. The darkness of this place combined with the darkness inside of me are almost too much to bear. It makes me feel vulnerable in a way I can hardly understand—and Grievous laughs at it. He chokes out a guttural cackle, mocking everything I am.

But I cut his maniacal glee short with one final swing of my lightsaber. I drive my blade through him, just as he drove his into my mother. Grievous, silent now, tumbles back into the darkness, and I know without having to see that he's vanished.

Despite besting my enemy, destroying him just as I'd dreamed of destroying him for so long, I feel nothing. There's no satisfaction. Nothing inside of me is different. I'm still consumed by the same fury.

It's just as Grievous—or the specter assuming his form—said it would be.

I scream into the nothingness that surrounds me.

The prize I seek is close. I can feel its dark power beckoning me. Soon, very soon, I will unlock the Sith mysteries from a time long forgotten, and I'll be able to use this knowledge to destroy my enemies—and anyone else who stands opposed to me.

I enter a long corridor that leads to an unremarkable door at the other end. I know, immediately, this is my destination. The answers I seek are just beyond that threshold.

On each side of the corridor, there are more statues, similar to the ones I saw earlier. But these figures are armored instead of cloaked, though their faces remain concealed. They resemble the warriors I saw in the paintings, and I can't help wondering what wars were fought on this distant planet so many years ago.

Though intrigued by the statues, I keep my focus sharp. If this place has taught me anything, it's to expect unusual, unexplainable things to happen. Dim light from outside comes in through a narrow row of windows on each side of the corridor, and the shadows that the statues cast are long and dark. Anything can be hidden within them.

I proceed cautiously, peering into the darkness. I'm unafraid. Whether this place is trying to test me or taunt me, I don't know. What I do know is that I won't be driven back by the treacherous obstacles it has to offer.

When I reach the end of the corridor, I begin to wonder if I've seen the last of the castle's games. If I've proven myself worthy of whatever Sith legacy awaits beyond this door.

But when I open the door and step inside the room on the other side, I realize the games are far from over.

A long-haired man is in the center of the room, down on his knees, completely still. I know this pose. I know this man.

The *Jedi*—Qui-Gon Jinn.

"We meet again," he says, remaining in his meditative pose.

"Master Jedi," I say, entering fully. The room is small and unadorned, yet I feel the power within nonetheless. It radiates beneath my feet, and I know this is where I am meant to be.

"You've traveled a great distance to be here," the Jedi says.

I laugh at his assessment. "Not as great as you, considering you're no longer among the living."

The Jedi smiles then rises to his feet. He folds his arms into the sleeves of his robes.

"And you came all this way, to what?" I ask. "To fight once more? I defeated you once already; I am perfectly happy to do it again."

"That's where you're wrong," he says. "You did kill me, that much is true. But I was never defeated simply because I lost our duel."

"How I *hate* every word that comes out of the mouths of you Jedi," I growl.

I begin to circle him, waiting for him to move for his lightsaber. That's why he's here, is it not? Our paths converge for one final battle. But the Jedi makes no such move. He simply stands there, radiating a calm that I so despise.

"Why are you here?" I finally ask.

"I'm here to offer you a choice, Maul. I want you to leave this castle, forget that it exists, and take your first step on the path toward a different destiny."

"I see," I say, containing my disgust for the Jedi— or whatever he is—long enough to learn the meaning of his cryptic words. "And what path is this—the path of the Jedi?"

The Jedi smiles, almost scoffing at me. "I thought you were above such narrow considerations—Jedi and Sith, light and dark. There's more to this galaxy than that."

My gaze narrows as I study my opponent. He

makes an interesting point, particularly for a Jedi. "Then what would you have me do?"

"Free yourself of the prison of your own making."

I stop dead in my tracks and grip the hilt of my weapon. I'm close enough to ignite it and cut the Jedi down in one simple movement.

"And what do you know of me or this supposed prison?" I ask. My breathing becomes labored as I feel my anger start to return. Although I wonder, in the moment, if it is ever really gone.

"I know that you are ruled by your need for revenge against everyone who's wronged you," the Jedi says. "But if I might ask: What good will it do you if you kill your enemies? When Kenobi and Sidious are gone, like me, where will that leave you?"

"Listen to you, festering in your mediocrity. I *defeated* you. And even if I hadn't, Darth Sidious would have driven a blade into your back in due time, just as he did all the Jedi. And yet you think you know the path that is right for me?"

"You still haven't answered my question, Maul," the Jedi says. "If you quench your thirst for revenge, who will you become?"

As the Jedi speaks, my hold on my lightsaber slackens. I even smile a bit. "No," I say. "I see what you are doing, Master Jedi. Like Savage and like Grievous, you're trying to taunt me. You want me to unleash my anger—but why?"

Now the Jedi does scoff. "You and I both know it's not anger that you feel."

As quickly as I managed to regain my poise, I feel it start to slip away. "You know *nothing* of what I feel."

"All your losses—your mother, your brother, your place at your master's side. You don't have to be ashamed."

I ignite my lightsaber and feel its satisfying hum pulsing in my hand. The light from my crimson blades fills the room. "I feel nothing but fury and hatred— fueled by people like *you*."

Why won't this Jedi move? He simply stands there,

bathed in the light of my blades. He hasn't reached for his own weapon.

I'm overwhelmed by the need for him to fight me, but I also must know the reason for his torments.

"You feel pain," the Jedi says. "And while your anger may be the weapon you use to destroy others, your pain will be the weapon that is used to destroy *you.*"

"Why?" I ask as I dig my feet into the ground, readying to lash out. "Why do you taunt me with your simpleminded judgments?"

The Jedi bows his head. He breathes deep then looks back up, focuses his eyes on mine, and says: "Because your desire to cause pain in others will never heal your own. I need you to understand that your destiny is yours to decide. And when that persistent weakness of yours becomes your final failure, it will wound you deeper than any lightsaber could."

I erupt. Moving as if compelled by a power beyond even my control, I leap toward the Jedi and strike.

Again and again and again, I attack with my blades, yelling out as I do. All I can see is red as the light of my weapon obscures my vision.

By the time I stop, I'm panting. I swallow hard and realize that the Jedi is no longer there; he never was. I was slashing, uselessly, against the air. The realization, and the exertion I spent, leaves me empty.

I also no longer feel the dark power that drew me to this room in the first place. It's gone. I search in vain for something, anything that will aid me in my quest. I push against the bare walls, desperate to find a hidden wall or chamber, something that will reveal a relic of some kind, or a book with arcane knowledge.

But there's nothing. I came all this way for *nothing*.

As I board my ship, I'm tempted by the thought of assaulting the castle as I fly overhead and leveling it to dust. The gesture, though, would be a pointless one.

The castle, whether standing or reduced to ash, is none of my concern.

What is my concern is the path ahead. The galaxy holds many, many more mysteries. There are other dark secrets to be found. Other Sith temples to explore.

I take my seat in the cockpit and chart a new course.

My quest for vengeance continues.

BLOOD MOON UPRISING

VERA STRANGE

Tsukimitsurin

Jungle Moon—Mid Rim

Imperial Refinery

"LORD VADER, we are clear for landing."

With that proclamation, the Imperial shuttle descended from the hazy reddish sky and landed with a great hiss in front of the Imperial refinery.

Flanked by stormtroopers clutching blasters, Commander Das Erdol rushed out from the plant to greet the newly arrived ship. She was about the same height as the troopers in their white armor, meaning that she was on the taller side, but her face wasn't concealed. She had gray eyes, dark skin, and white-blonde hair tied back in a tight bun.

The troopers marched in unison, their boots sinking into the loamy ground and trailing matching lines of blood-red footprints. The crimson hue was due to the heavy iron content in the soil, one of the many reasons this remote moon, with its wealth of untouched natural resources, remained of great value to the Empire.

Tsukimitsurin was mostly unpopulated, aside from a few tribes of locals, making the true inhabitants of the moon the flora and fauna. The jungle was host to an array of species, some harmless but many lethal. The locals had a saying—"Stay out of the vines."

It was a fair warning.

One she should have heeded.

Erdol knew the dangers that lurked in the thick trees that shrouded this moon, which was supposed to be under her "command," as the Empire had claimed it. But the wildness defied all attempts at subjugation.

And it fought back, when needed.

Unconsciously, Erdol glanced down at her forearm, where her uniform concealed a deep scar cut into her flesh, a nice parting gift from her first expedition into the jungle after she took over this command post. She could still remember the creature's hideous snarls.

The half-dragon, half-jungle-cat predator—a chimeraleon—had paid with its life. The creature, native to this moon, had a coat that shifted colors to blend seamlessly into the trees and vines, lizard-like speed and agility that allowed it to climb, and razor-sharp jaws that breathed fire. Before succumbing to blaster fire, it left lasting damage to tendon and nerve and flesh.

However, sometimes the most important lessons scarred you. She wouldn't forget this one.

"Stand back," Commander Erdol ordered the stormtroopers as they came to a halt in front of the shuttle, which gave nothing away. The ship sat idling, but its bay doors remained closed tight. Even the pilots were invisible to her eyes through the tinted windows.

She waited in a rigid military stance for what came next or, more accurately, who would emerge from the elegant ship. Such shuttles often transported high-ranking officials and dignitaries, but also troopers and cargo. Regardless, this visit to her remote industrial outpost was highly unusual and also unexpected, and that made her nervous.

No, more than nervous.

It terrified her down to her bones.

She knew it couldn't be anything good.

Behind her, the metal and steel of the refinery stood out in stark contrast to the moon's lush greenery and natural beauty. Two suns illuminated the sky, each at half mast, signaling that it was already midafternoon, though dusk still remained a way off.

The air was sweltering and humid, which made it hard to breathe and impossible for Erdol not to sweat profusely under her stiff gray Imperial uniform and narrow brimmed hat. She fidgeted with the collar, wishing for any relief from the heat.

But it would not come.

She should have grown used to the tropical climate by then, but it was the polar opposite of her icy homeworld in the Outer Rim. Every night, she still dreamed of snow.

Whoosh.

Slowly, deliberately, the boarding ramp lowered from the hull of the shuttle and touched down on the ground with a light thud. The sudden movement startled the commander. Steam gushed from the idling engines, camouflaging the ramp in a thick fog.

Erdol strained to see through it. But soon she realized she could hear him before she could see him.

Inhale. Pause. Exhale.

The sound of artificial breathing pierced the fog

like blaster fire. Instantly, Erdol tensed up, feeling shocked to her core. Suddenly—

With a great swishing of his black cape, Darth Vader himself strode down the ramp, materializing like a wraith from the vapor. He traveled alone.

The unblinking eyes of his helmet immediately locked on to the commander. Their reflective sheen mirrored the red sky, flickering with the blazing fire of the two suns.

Erdol stared back at the Sith Lord in shock. How could this be? What was Darth Vader doing there? Of all places?

Not only was this visit a surprise, but it was also the first time she had been in the presence of the mysterious Sith Lord, as she was merely the lowly commander of an out-of-the-way outpost, not even an admiral or general.

But all at once, it became clear that the stories did not do Darth Vader justice. In real life, Vader was a far more imposing figure, as if terror wafted from his mechanical suit like the vaporous exhaust oozing from his ship.

"Lord Vader . . . we were not expecting you," Erdol managed to choke out, wringing her hands and taking in the Sith Lord's dark visage.

Vader remained silent.

Too silent.

His unmoving facade gave nothing away. Only his artificial breathing pierced the muggy air. Commander Erdol felt compelled to fill the void.

"W-with all due respect, my lord," she stammered on foolishly, "what brings you to our humble industrial outpost on Tsukimitsurin?"

Still Vader did not respond. Instead, he marched right past Commander Erdol and her troops so she had to jog to keep up. Everything Vader did had great purpose. Matching his long intentional strides, his cape swished around his ankles.

Vader headed toward the entrance of the refinery, huge steel double doors that protected the plant's vulnerable innards. Overhead, smokestacks spewed filthy exhaust into the air, while wastewater streamed away below, dumping into the raging rivers that cut through the otherwise impenetrable jungle.

Stormtroopers guarded the perimeter walls, armed with blasters, and droids zipped around and beeped, delivering supplies and communications. Imperial workers handled the pumps, their faces blackened with soot and oil. Some looked over with interest, then quickly turned back to their work lest the Dark Lord find them to be slacking in their duties.

Vader swept his gaze over the plant and took everything in. Erdol could sense that nothing escaped his notice. Finally, as she caught up to him by the doors, Darth Vader spoke.

"Commander, your refinery is operating behind schedule," Vader said in his imposing deep voice. It was as much a weapon as the silence that had preceded it. He wielded both with extreme control and precision, just like his lightsaber.

"Lord Vader, with all due respect," Erdol replied, trying to keep her voice steady but failing miserably, "you cannot expect miracles. We're running the refinery pumps day and night to meet the needs of the Imperial fleet. That requires enormous energy to power them."

Vader did not break stride, nor did he wait for an invitation, continuing onward into the plant. Inside, it stunk of oil and chemicals. He kept walking at a fast clip through the plant, and the commander had to rush to keep up. Droids zipped around, beeping when they almost collided with Vader. One sharp look sent them scurrying away in alarm.

"Commander, I do not share your appraisal of the situation," Vader continued, scanning the machines that labored to transform the slick black oil pumped from underground into fuel cells to power the Empire's ever-growing fleet of battleships.

"My lord, I cannot invent more hours in the day," Erdol went on in a shaky voice. "Perhaps if we could have extra supplies, more workers—"

Vader cut her off, his voice filled with barely contained fury. "Commander Erdol, your excuses are both inept and insipid." His face, beneath the black mask, was of course unreadable. Only his breath continued to hiss in and out with mechanical precision.

The entire effect was unnerving.

"I am displeased with your production," Vader went on. "And your explanations are lacking. Your plant is being sabotaged—right under your nose."

Erdol's jaw went slack. "But . . . how can you know that? I've had no reports of disturbances or anything amiss."

"We captured a rebel spy who, after much persuasion, confessed to their treacherous plan for this moon," Vader replied. He stared down at her. "Perhaps if you weren't as blind as you are stupid, you would have noticed it for yourself."

"No, that's impossible," Erdol said, grasping for any explanation but falling short. "I can assure you, the perimeter is secure. I've recently doubled patrols. Reinforced security protocols. Set up . . . checkpoints . . . and curfews . . ."

The commander's voice became strangled. She cried out and clutched at her throat, clawing at the invisible hand constricting her windpipe and crushing it.

Vader continued to stare at her. His fist was clenched.

Finally, right when Erdol was about to lose consciousness and suffocate to death, Vader flicked his hand and released her from the invisible steel grip.

The commander collapsed, gasping for breath.

"Commander, your mind is weak and you lack imagination," Vader went on, staring down at her through his black helmet. His breath hissed in and out, punctuating his words. "You have failed the Emperor for the first—and last time."

"But . . . my lord . . . who is behind this treachery?" Erdol gasped in a raspy voice. "The locals have expressed some resistance . . . but we dealt with them harshly. Perhaps we could dispatch more troops to *remind* them who's in charge—"

"Commander, this is clearly beyond your abilities," Vader said, stroking the hilt of his lightsaber. "Leave it to me. If the rebels are here, then we must flush them out. The Empire cannot be seen as weak. The traitors must be destroyed."

Vader turned away and strode toward the doors with great purpose, his black cape sweeping around his ankles. He paused, glancing back at Erdol.

"I will deal with you later," Vader said in an unflinching tone. "You can account for your failures then."

Darth Vader stalked the rebels through the jungle.

He went alone, able to move with more stealth and speed when not hampered by the clumsy machinations of stormtroopers, not to mention that worthless commander of theirs. He would deal with *her* the next day.

The rebel traitors will be flushed out, Vader thought as he slashed ahead, *and punished for their treachery*. Nobody evaded him, not once he had them in his sights.

The jungle was thick and undisturbed, but Vader used his lightsaber to cut through the brush, slicing through vines and branches with the flickering red blade. He used both the Force and his suit's sensors to track the rebels.

He followed his instincts, knowing to trust where they led him. He continued cutting a path through the foliage, but suddenly—

Something *large* stirred in the trees.

Vader froze, his hand clutching the hilt of his lightsaber.

He listened closely but also felt outward with his

abilities, searching the disturbance out through the vines. This always gave him the extra edge, which this poor foolish creature could not possibly know.

With a ferocious growl, the camouflaged beast leapt at him from the trees—all snarls, claws, and fire-spewing jaws.

It was a chimeraleon.

Vader savored the moment. He wished it would last longer.

Then, in one swift motion, he whipped around and slashed at the half-cat, half-dragon predator with his lightsaber. The red blade flickered and spit.

Slash, slash, slash.

Three quick strokes.

Blazing red light. Sparks flying and sizzling at the humidity in the air.

But the chimeraleon dodged the blows with agile feline movements. It crouched and spun, whipping its spiked lizard tail at him.

Everything about the chimeraleon was deadly, from its spiny tail to its razor-sharp jaws that could breathe fire.

But Vader was not afraid. He stood his ground.

The creature's sharp feline eyes locked on to Vader. The creature did not blink. Its ever-shifting mane, now a pattern of emerald and green to match the foliage, spiked up in warning. They stared each other down like that—

One predator versus another.

It felt like an eternity but really lasted mere seconds. Vader did not relent. The beast growled and scampered up the trunk of the nearest tree, ready to attack again. It could climb quickly with its massive claws, and that gave the creature an advantage in a typical fight, and its hide blended perfectly into the thick jungle, rendering it virtually invisible to the naked eye.

Vader waited, scanning the thick foliage for any movement.

Roar!

Suddenly, the beast unleashed a ferocious growl and leapt at Vader. The claws slashed out, easily able to slit his throat or disembowel him. Its jaws cracked open to reveal razor-sharp teeth. A blast of fiery breath shot out at him as the creature flew through the air.

But Vader did not duck or retreat.

Instead, he aimed for the heart and plunged his lightsaber into the beast. The speed and ferocity with which the chimeraleon had launched its attack also proved to be its demise.

The momentum drove the lightsaber in deep.

The chimeraleon collapsed next to Vader with one last pitiful squeal that reverberated through the jungle. The lightsaber protruded from its chest. It shuddered once, twice, then fell still. A flock of birds took off, streaking through the sky with a great fluttering of wings.

Vader nudged the limp body with his boot.

Pity the creature didn't last longer.

Then he retracted his lightsaber from the body and peered down at his prey. The jungle had fallen silent, as if in mourning for the mighty predator dead in its midst.

Darth Vader continued tracking the rebels, even as the suns began to wilt in the sky.

Slash, slash, slash.

The jungle grew darker and felt more ominous. His lightsaber forged a path through the thick vegetation. He could *feel* he was getting closer to their trail. He waded through a small stream, which gathered strength the deeper it cut into the jungle. He followed it.

Soon it became a raging river. Vader pushed onward through the jungle without slowing as he hunted the rebels. They would not escape him, he knew. He would flush them out.

His efforts were soon rewarded.

Vader spotted a clearing in the jungle straight ahead. He marched toward it, pushing his way through the ropey vines that hung from the trees.

He scanned the clearing. This was an encampment. Better yet, it showed signs of recent habitation—cookstove, bedroll imprints, fresh footprints in the red soil. And one other thing, accidentally left behind and forgotten.

Vader picked up the discarded helmet with a blast shield.

It was marked by the red rebel insignia.

Despite the commander's feeble protests, the plant falling behind schedule wasn't simple incompetence, negligence, or the work of local saboteurs. As Vader suspected—*rebels*.

He followed a set of footprints in the soil that led deeper into the jungle. They were large and clearly not human. This drew his interest. He tracked them, moving quietly and carefully this time. The element of surprise could prove a valuable weapon when wielded appropriately.

That was when—

He spotted *her* in the jungle.

Well, he felt her through the Force before he saw her, in quick succession. A flash of white fur. A gentle rustling of vines. The soft clomp of cushioned footsteps.

Vader crouched down and watched her focused movements, feeling for her energy at the same time. The Wookiee girl was tall, covered head to toe in a thick shaggy coat of white fur. Sharp canines protruded from her jowls, one of the hallmarks of her kind.

Surprisingly, Vader realized that she was only a youngling, the equivalent of a human teenager. Intelligence oozed from her mind—and also her name.

Kataarynnna.

Vader held still, secreted in the lush vegetation, and

watched her closely. His hand moved to the hilt of his lightsaber, though he did not draw it yet.

The Wookiee girl crouched by a small power generator that straddled the river with steel supports. She worked alone. Through these generators, wires connected the refinery to the main hydropower station, which sported a large dam that harnessed the raging river to generate energy to power the pumps.

The Wookiee girl glanced around to make sure she wasn't being watched, unaware that Vader already had her in his sights. Then she bent down and pulled something from her rough canvas bag. She planted an improvised explosive device by the power generator. She quickly armed it and stood up, clutching an object in her scruffy hand.

A detonator.

That was when she jerked her head around.

Her eyes locked on him and widened with fear.

Kataarynnna immediately took off, racing through

the jungle as fast as her long legs would carry her. Despite her remarkable height and size, she was lithe and agile, as if she was born of the trees. She sprinted ahead with impressive speed and grace, leaping over trunks and whipping through the thick vines obscuring her path.

Vader chased after her, bursting from the jungle. Although his movements were more plodding and deliberate, he ran with great force and never, ever tired.

But the Wookiee girl's strength and clear familiarity with the local terrain gave her a slight edge, and she remained ahead of him . . . for now.

But it wouldn't last.

A surge of anger erupted in Vader's chest. It flowed through him, white-hot and searing. He savored it and channeled it into his movements, unsheathing his lightsaber and using it to slash through the vines and increase his speed. Anger was his power generator.

Vader could see the Wookiee girl just ahead.

White fur and churning long legs.

Somehow, she managed to run even faster. Vader could sense that she had a specific destination in her mind. And also a clear purpose—and that was to destroy it.

But she clouded his vision. Her mind was strong, Vader realized, much stronger than any he had encountered in some time. He pushed harder, trying to force her mind back open.

He caught a quick flash—

The hydropower station.

Vader pried the image from her thoughts before her mind locked down again. She might have a strong will, but he was stronger.

They were nearing the hydropower station. Vader could hear it before he could see it. The roar of the river gave it away. The Wookiee girl burst from the jungle first—but Vader was right behind her. The station's steel-and-permacrete structure resembled an imposing fortress rising out of the jungle. The sound of the water flowing through the dam was almost deafening.

Stormtroopers protected and patrolled the perimeter wall.

They spotted the Wookiee girl.

"Look out, a trespasser!" one trooper called to the others. They turned around and raised their blasters. And opened fire—

Shots hissed down at her.

But the Wookiee girl ducked behind the dam that caged the river, holding back its powerful flow. Blaster fire ricocheted off the permacrete dangerously close to her head, but she crouched and planted the last of her explosives right at the base of the dam.

She reached down, dodging blaster shots, and armed it with a soft beep.

The red light flashed its warning.

So this is her plan, Vader thought as he strode forth and emerged from the jungle. Destroy their hydropower source, thus bringing the refinery's pumps to a screeching halt and cutting off the Empire's valuable fuel supplies.

She didn't yet know it, but her plan was foiled.

Nobody could escape him.

"Call for reinforcements!" the stormtroopers communicated, then rushed down from the perimeter wall to back up their commander. But Vader raised his gloved hand.

The Wookiee girl was trapped, caught between Vader and the troopers, her back against the permacrete barrier of the dam. She was alone and had nowhere left to run.

"Hold your fire," Vader commanded.

The troopers followed orders, coming around to flank him with their blasters while Vader clutched his lightsaber. He illuminated it with one quick flick of his hand.

The red blade sputtered with menace.

The Wookiee girl looked fearful and tried to retreat farther, but her back scraped against the wall.

She held up her scruffy hand, which still clutched the detonator.

Her jaws opened, and she spoke in the guttural growls and whines of her native language, Shyriiwook, but her message was clear enough.

"Stay back—or I'll destroy the generators," she growled.

She had skills, this rebel. Vader was intrigued. He pushed deeper into her mind using the Force. Fear loosened her grip, made it easier for him to pry it open. This girl was the mastermind behind the sabotage. Even at her young age, she was already a formidable rebel leader.

He caught flashes of her life.

Despite the relatively short span in the long life of her kind, pain and torment filled it almost from the moment of her birth. Her hatred for the Empire burned with searing fire.

Orphan.

The word ricocheted through her head like a blaster

shot. So they were the same in that, then. Vader understood the rage she carried.

"Your thoughts betray you—and your foolish plan," Vader said in his deep voice. "Anger and hatred are powerful weapons. Your talents could be put to better use by the Empire. Pity you're wasting them fighting for weak rebel traitors."

Kataarynnna understood him, and her anger flared white-hot.

Vader pressed at her mind with the Force. He showed her the power she could wield if she joined forces with the Empire. Power, domination, and control, restoring order to the galaxy. For a moment, it seemed that she would give in and surrender.

But then—

She pushed him out, closing her mind like a steel cage.

"Never," she growled. It echoed off the dam, louder than even the raging river.

"This is your last chance," Vader said in a menacing voice, raising his lightsaber to strike her down with one swift blow and end her life. "You are beaten. It is useless to resist. You underestimate the power of the Empire."

Kataarynnna stared him down. Her growls echoed out as she pounded her chest.

Her tone and posture made her message clear.

"I'll die first."

"As you wish," Vader said with disdain.

Vader prepared to swing his lightsaber at her. She didn't stand a chance against his power—but she had one last hope. She clung to it fiercely as she raised her fist.

A flash of metal.

The detonator.

Kataarynnna moved to press it, triggering the explosive devices she'd planted around the power generators. The explosion would surely kill her, but it was clear she didn't care. This would be her sacrifice for the Rebellion, for this ravaged moon.

She pressed down on the button—

But *nothing* happened.

No explosions rocked the generators. The dam held fast against the raging river. She tried again, futilely pressing at the detonator. But the button remained fixed in place.

Shock and horror washed over her features as all hope leached away, along with her last defense.

Satisfaction flowed through Vader. He lifted up his fist. He had beaten her to it, using the Force to jam the detonator before she could set it off.

"You underestimate the power of the dark side," he said. "And now you shall die for it."

He swung his lightsaber to strike her down while simultaneously reaching out with the Force to fully crush the detonator in her hand and render it useless.

But then—

Something drew Vader's attention. He paused mid-stroke and whipped his head around. Rustling noises emerged from the jungle. He focused in on the disturbance. Footsteps crushing the brush. And whispered voices and whining growls.

Quickly, Vader released his Force hold on the detonator and jerked around while stormtroopers swarmed over to back him up. They aimed their blasters at the trees.

Everything went still for a long moment. And then—

Rebel forces poured from the jungle—a group of older Wookiees and human rebel fighters in combat gear and helmets. This was an ambush. The Wookiee girl had lured Vader into a trap.

Fury rushed through Vader.

He would make her suffer.

"Save the girl!" one rebel yelled before firing a shot their way. "Get the detonator!"

The rebels unleashed a barrage of blaster fire on Vader and the troopers, trying to push them back from the girl and rescue her. The shots lit up the jungle with fire and noise. The Wookiees fought with their hand-carved wooden long-gun rifles and bowcasters—a sort of laser crossbow—while the rebel soldiers fired standard blasters.

They exchanged fire with the stormtroopers as Vader wielded his lightsaber to deflect their shots and push them back into the jungle and away from the vulnerable hydropower station. The explosive flashed with red light. It was still armed. One good blast could ignite it.

A few rebel soldiers took fire and fell to the ground with pained cries, while several troopers also took hits. They screamed out and clutched at their chests, toppling over. Their white armor peppered the ground, standing out against the red-stained soil.

But Vader could not be taken down so easily.

Almost single-handedly, he drove the rebels back toward the jungle, using his lightsaber to intercept the blaster fire and send it flying back at them.

"No, watch out!" one rebel cried as a shot ricocheted back on him.

He collapsed to the ground. But many still remained standing.

Vader reached out with the Force, pulling branches from the trees and hurling them at the rebels. They ducked and dove out of the way as the debris buried them.

The rebels were losing ground . . . quickly.

Vader drove them back to the edge of the jungle. They would soon be defeated. He fought harder, whipping his lightsaber and hurling rocks and boulders at them.

In the chaos of the melee, the Wookiee girl managed to escape and joined the rebel reinforcements. She was still holding the detonator. Distracted by the ambush, Vader had released his hold on the device and failed to fully crush it.

She went to push the button—

But Vader sensed her intention and fought back with the Force. The rebels fired at him, hoping to break his concentration, while Kataarynnna resisted, trying to depress the button.

It was a battle of wills—light versus dark.

But Vader pushed harder.

With one last tremendous effort, he crushed the detonator in her hands. The metal crumpled, rendered useless. He had won the battle. However, the explosive power from their battle of wills tore a rift in the ground beneath them.

Crack!

The ground split open before him and dropped away, creating a deep crevice that separated Vader from the rebels. He stood on one side, they on the other.

Vader watched with barely contained fury. Their

plan foiled, the rebels quickly fled into the jungle, escaping on camouflaged speeder bikes and Wookiee catamarans. They melted away into the dense vegetation, quickly vanishing from view.

The stormtroopers continued to fire at them, taking down a few rebel speeders, which crashed in the jungle with fiery explosions. But many still managed to escape.

Then something unexpected happened.

Kataarynnna circled back on her speeder bike. Her eyes shone with determination. She stared Vader down. She accelerated faster and faster, gaining speed and heading for the rift.

She jumped her speeder over it.

Zooooom.

She whizzed toward Vader, dodging blaster fire, and circled around toward the hydropower station. She aimed for the explosive set at the base of the dam.

Vader raised his lightsaber, swiping at her bike. He cut off one of the blasters, but she pivoted away so that one blaster remained operational. She struggled to keep the bike steady.

She fired . . . it was a perfect shot.

Kaboom!

A huge explosion rocked the dam. Cracks broke the permacrete barrier. As water leaked through it, those cracks grew bigger. The river broke free, escaping and flooding the jungle. Even the trees seemed to sigh in relief as the water saturated their soil and quenched their thirst. Torn asunder by the escaping water, the hydropower station collapsed in a pile of dust and ruin.

Vader watched as the Wookiee girl raced away on her speeder bike, back into the jungle, escaping with the other rebel traitors.

Still clutching his lightsaber, which flickered in the dimming light as the two suns set on the horizon, Vader stood at the edge of the rift in the ground while the ruins of the hydropower station settled behind him. Anger flowed through him like the raging river soaking the jungle.

How dare she defy the Empire? For that, she would pay.

This battle wasn't the end.

This was merely the beginning of a longer war. Now Vader knew about *her*. She wasn't safe. He wouldn't forget her and her treachery. In fact, she would never be safe again.

Vader looked up. The horizon was streaked blood red with the brilliant sunset. Dust obscured the light, drifting from the rubble. His artificial breath hissed in and out.

"There is no escape from the Empire," Vader said to the sky, to the setting suns, to the Wookiee girl speeding away through the jungle. "I will hunt you down—and destroy you."

His thoughts carried great power. They radiated out, broadcast with the strength of the Force. He knew that she could *feel* his intention, the malice he held for her.

Vader would be back. And he would come with reinforcements and be prepared. She wouldn't get away so easily again. Nobody could escape from Darth Vader.

Next time he would *finish* her.

LUKE ON THE BRIGHT SIDE

SAM MAGGS

IT'S NOT THAT I'M AFRAID of the dark. It's really not.

Unfamiliar? Sure. You grow up on a planet with two suns and three moons, you get used to blinding days and still-bright nights. If anything, suns-set is a relief on Tatooine, not something to worry about. Ghomrassen, Guermessa, and Chenini reflect only light from the suns, not heat. The day's blistering temperatures fade away into the hazy sort of half-light of the evening, and it's suddenly . . . freeing. The sand stops burning your feet; you don't have to squint to see farther than the tip of your nose; you might not even dehydrate.

Well, you won't dehydrate as quickly, anyway.

No. You want something hidden on Tatooine—secreted away somewhere—you don't rely on the flimsy cover of "darkness." There's oceans of sand dunes for that, and they're even easier to get lost in at the peak of daylight than they are in the middle of the night. You can't trust your own brain in the dunes in the middle of the day. Now *that's* scary.

So it's not really something I grew up thinking about. I've only experienced darkness as a pilot. But that's different, too; that's *real* darkness, the kind that reminds you that what you're not seeing isn't even there. Nothing's hiding in the shadows in deep space; there *are* no shadows. There's just . . . nothing at all. That kind of blackness is empty and, in a strange way, predictable. The darkness is the least scary part of space. The truly terrifying stuff shows up to interrupt the dark: asteroids, solar flares, Star Destroyers.

And it's a freeing kind of darkness, too, almost in the same way as on Tatooine. That space is there, just waiting for you to exist in it. It doesn't fight against you like sand beneath your feet; your ship slices right through it, with no effort. You could cut the engines and keep flying and flying through that darkness forever. It'll never try to stop you. It can't.

Here, on the other hand . . .

This darkness is *not* freeing. This darkness is . . . extremely the opposite of that.

"Luke?" A voice, out of the constricting dark. To my right. Left? Definitely left.

"Reyé?" I call out in return, throwing my hands out in front of me blindly. "Where are you?" I start groping around, and my hands quickly make contact with a wall of snow and ice centimeters from my outstretched fingertips. So, not forward, then. Got it.

It's not that I'm afraid. It's just that if I'm down here for one more second, suffocating in this blackness that I think I'll probably never escape and this is the place that I'm going to die and no one's even going to find me because it's so ridiculously *dark*, I'm going to rip my own face off using the Force.

I don't even think the Force can do that. But if any-one can find a way, it's me, right now.

Wait . . . *the Force.* No one can see me roll my eyes at myself, but I do it anyway. It's enough to know I did it, because in that moment, I deserved it.

"Over here!" Reyé shouts back. That's not very helpful, admittedly, but he's been so helpful to me since I arrived on the base that I can hardly hold it against him. I can't see it right now, but he does have a very nice smile.

"Stay still!" I brace myself against the packed-snow wall with my hands and close my eyes entirely out of habit—it's not like it makes things any darker. I take a deep breath in and let it out slowly, emptying my mind. And then again. And then again.

My back itches. I ease it. I swallow really loudly, for some reason. I ignore it. I feel the real and imag-ined pressure of the icy cave-in directly above me, and I push it out of my mind. I focus. I *really* focus.

And suddenly, it's like fireworks. My awareness

rolls out from me like the desert wind across the sand, mapping out the world around me without needing light or touch or smell or any of it. It flows out over ice shards and snow and debris piles, tracing a chart through the closed-off tunnel around me. The Force lights up the backs of my eyelids with sensation and information, pouring in from all sides at full speed.

And *there*, six meters to my left—black combat boots; water-resistant pants in the same white material as his fur-trimmed parka; a dark beard over even darker skin; a standard-order helmet and goggles covering curly hair that the Force somehow tells me is very soft and smells very good—there he is. Sergeant Reyé Hollis, Alliance Special Forces.

More like Alliance Special Forced to Hang Out with Me. I know he can't stand me.

And now I'm the reason we're trapped in an ice cave-in underneath Echo Base on Hoth, where we're both going to die.

Great.

It didn't have to go this way.

"I'm finding you!" I hear Luke shout from a ways down the tunnel. I roll my eyes, even though there's no one around to notice. Where else am I going to go? Coruscant? Has the flyboy not noticed that we're stuck here?

And what, he's "finding" me? With his wibbly magic crockery? It's going to take him longer to *feel* where I am with his *heart* or whatever it is that Jedi do than it would take me to march a couple of meters down the tunnel and smack him on the shoulder. What a waste of time and energy. Still, there's no arguing with Luke. I know better than that already, and I only met him earlier today.

It's not even that dark down here.

And it isn't that I don't like the guy. He seems fine. A little full of himself, in that head-in-the-stars kind of way. But he's got great hair. Eyes real blue, too, like the sky over this icy rock on a clear day. It's just that, in every story about them I've ever heard, Jedi are pointless and useless at best, and harmful and dangerous at worst, and there's no need to bring that whole thing back.

That's all.

With a sigh, I get down onto the snowy floor of the cave—tunnel? Tunnel-cave? It *was* a tunnel; now it's a cave—and pull my knees up under my chin. Easier to preserve body heat if you're as small as you can get. At least that's what the info-holo said on the way over here. I have time to kill while I wait for the Jedi Genius to stumble his way over to me with his eyes closed, so I think back to a few hours ago—right around the time we first met.

I was busy doing my job. Because I have a job. A *real* one.

See, after the Battle of Yavin—before the blown-up pieces of the Death Star even had a chance to cool, I'd say—we rebels were on the run again. Had to evac

Yavin 4. We've never been able to stay in one place very long. Empire always comes after us, one way or another. We had to find a new base camp, and as fast as possible.

Eventually, General Rieekan and the other bigwigs in the Alliance settled on Hoth. Fine. It's no Canto Bight, but that's the whole point. It's not even on standard navigational star charts. About as hidden as hidden gets, in space. The plan is to stay here for a long, long time.

Only problem with Hoth is it's not exactly . . . hothpitable. Unless you're a tauntaun, I guess. The place is a giant ice cube. It's no wonder nobody ever bothered to map it; I can't think of a single reason anyone except the galaxy's most wanted would find this place appealing.

So this is where I've been with the rest of the hardworking Alliance crew. Day in, day out, digging tunnel after tunnel, cavern after cavern, through snow and ice with laser ice cutters. They found a mountain in the southern Clabburn Range perfect for hollowing out. Thousands of combat personnel and a whole whack of starfighters and transports need a whole lot of space, turns out. And don't let them tell you the plasmold insulation makes a difference in this kind of cold; I think I'll probably never feel the tips of my ears again. The end of my nose, either. Perma-numb.

Conditions like that have a tendency to bond you to the folks around you. Got real close with the rest of the Hoth squad. I even know a gal who claims she came up with the name Echo Base, on account of the way your voice seems to travel and travel through these frozen halls.

And then, earlier today, in strode Luke Skywalker. The new Jedi, the Hero of Yavin himself. And he needed a babysitter.

"Skywalker?" I shouted, coming up behind the

new guy at a jog. We were standing in what was soon going to be the lower-level barracks, and the constant bass-heavy drone of the laser cutter blared on.

Didn't seem like he heard me. Luke was just staring at the wall of ice in front of him, looking up and up and up. His shaggy hair brushed the back of his coat collar; he wasn't even wearing a hat. He'd learn quick. We all did.

"Skywalker!" I repeated, louder this time, and right behind him, trying to get his attention. Luke's posture changed for a second; I was sure he was going to say something.

But instead, almost too fast for me to catch it, Luke spun on his heels and nabbed something out of the air with his gloved hand—something so small I could barely see it. After examining what was between his fingers for a moment, he looked up at me with a smile brighter than the sun reflecting off the ice outside.

"Glacier fly!" he yelled over the noise, holding his

palm open toward me. I looked down into his hand. Sure enough, there was a tiny little ice-looking bug sitting there calmly.

I didn't really know what to say. I decided on "Looks like it."

Luke nodded with all the seriousness in the galaxy. "I heard the fork-nosed ice worms native to the area used to live symbiotically with the glacier flies, before they all went extinct. Must have been a sight to see!" Suddenly, the laser cutter shut down, leaving a ringing silence in its wake. Into the emptiness, Luke said quietly, "Can you imagine?"

I blinked at him. "No." Then I stuck out my hand to match his. "Sergeant Reyé Hollis, Alliance Special Forces. I'm to familiarize you with Echo Base."

Luke looked at my hand, just for a second, before gently shaking his glacier fly free. He gripped my hand with a surprising strength and that same big smile. "Luke Skywalker. I'm here to help!"

I've always needed to be helpful. Mostly. "Of use." That's what my Aunt Beru liked to call me, in the sweetest way. She didn't have a not-sweet bone in her body.

(Her bones . . . Don't think about that.)

Anyway . . . it's what led me to the rebels, it's what got my torpedo into that little thermal exhaust port on the Death Star, and it's what brought me to Hoth. I like to have a purpose. Doesn't everyone? Isn't that something all people need, across space and time—Jedi or Sith, good or bad? Aren't we all just looking for our purpose in this big, empty, dark galaxy?

My purpose here on Hoth, at least at first, was to assist with the excavation of a particularly difficult system of tunnels the Alliance engineers and construction crew were boring into a mountainside. They'd been doing all right on their own, but it was slow work. It would be a lot easier if they had an easily transportable human sensor system to let them know where to dig and when.

Rebel leadership wouldn't hear it when I tried to tell them that I could barely explain what the Force was, let alone how it worked—or how to get it to work for me, reliably. But they sent me anyway. And now I have to try my best, for the sake of every soul on this base.

I couldn't exactly explain all that to my shockingly grumpy new base buddy, Reyé—Sergeant Hollis—as he marched me through the icy halls of Echo Base shortly after meeting, though, so I focused on the moment at hand. I thought the glacier fly was really neat. He, apparently, did not.

I was getting that from the fact that he hadn't said a word to me since we left the lower barracks.

"Where are you from, Sergeant?" I asked pleasantly, trying to break the silence in a way that wouldn't make either of us feel too awkward. We'd be spending a lot of time together down here; we might as well get to know each other.

He looked sidelong at me through thick dark lashes. "What, it's not obvious to you?"

"Well, I don't like to do that uninvited," I answered. "But if you're asking . . ."

I paused in the middle of the hall. It took Reyé a couple of steps before he realized I was no longer beside him, and he came to an abrupt halt. As he turned, I closed my eyes. Deep breaths. Wind over sand. Reaching out—I saw . . . and I felt . . .

"Ah!" My eyes flew open. "So much water, and so green. Your home is beautiful."

Reyé just stared at me. Really? I was sure I'd gotten it right. . . .

"I meant my name," he finally answered, his face inscrutable. "The *é* at the end of my name. 'S a Naboo thing. People sometimes know what planet I'm from, because of that."

I felt my face going red. "Right," I nodded, rushing to catch up with him as he started off with his long stride again. "Naboo. I've heard of that. For sure."

"Your first assignment is down this way." Reyé turned down a gently sloping corridor, taking us even deeper beneath the mountain. "No point in wasting time.

"That's what the Jedi always did, isn't it?" said Reyé dryly.

I shook my head in confusion. "What?"

"Waste time. Wave their hands around. Think real hard at stuff. Get people killed."

"No," I protested immediately. "No, it's not like that at all. It wasn't like that at all."

Reyé's eyebrows shot up. "No?" He gestured at the tunnel walls with his chin. "Then we're not here in the middle of the galaxy's worst ice cream shop prayin' every day that the Empire doesn't swoop down on us from above? 'Cause the Jedi got rid of all of the evil in the galaxy. Isn't that right?"

I swallowed and found my throat was as parched as if it were the middle of the day on Tatooine.

"No." I stared right in his dark and serious eyes and found a challenge waiting for me. "It didn't go that way, not last time. But this time, it's gonna be different. This time, you have me. And I won't let you down."

And then a giant fork-nosed ice worm shot through the icy ground next to us, and the entire world fell on our heads.

See, this is my problem with Jedi, right here. While the rest of us hardworking Alliance types have been busting our backs on this frozen Outer Rim rock for weeks, it's Luke Skywalker gets a medal and called a hero. As if he were the only one fighting at the Battle of Yavin. As if he were the most important person on this base.

It was always like that with the Jedi. From what I

heard, anyway. Show up, take the glory, leave things worse off than they were.

Hey, just like right now.

I squint into the near darkness and take in whatever my eyes can make out. That worm blasted through solid ice, collapsing the access tunnel around us. Entry and exit completely blocked. No way up or down. Best we've got to work with here is some busted-out lights and more ice.

Not ideal.

I watch Luke, eyes still closed, shuffling closer and closer to me, arms outstretched in front of him. I decide, mercifully in my opinion, to put the guy out of his misery, standing up and poking him in the chest before he can go any farther.

"Tag. You're it."

I can see the dim glint in Luke's eyes as they fly open. "Found you!"

Sure you did. "Yep. You sure did."

"We have to get out of here." Luke's breathing

pretty heavy, his eyes darting around wildly. Either he's claustrophobic, or he can't see well in the dark, or both. Either way, it's only a little bit funny. Mostly annoying, though.

"Whatever you do, don't use your space magic at it," I suggest, starting to feel around the icy walls for any gaps. "That's probably what woke it up."

I hear Luke let out something between a snort and an exhale behind me. "Oh, right. I'm sure it was the *Force* that woke it up, and not your *giant ice lasers.*"

"Giant ice lasers bring a lot of extinct animals back to life?" Do I feel air?

"Obviously not extinct!" Luke protests, grabbing the furry hood of my parka so he can trail me in the dark. "Because we just saw it! You know, I had a feeling, when I found that glacier fly. . . ."

Another eye roll in the dark. "A *feeling.*" Yep, definitely air. Right through this little gap . . .

"Yes, a *feeling,*" Luke mocks me right back. "You should try having one sometime."

Ugh. "Well, I'm *feeling* air," I say, yanking my hood forward and dragging the flyboy with it. Even in this pit I can still smell his shampoo. It's nice. Or whatever. "Put your hand here."

It only takes a second of watching Luke flail into the darkness before I grab his hand with an exasperated sigh and hold it over the small gap in the snow wall. Cold air—but flowing air; that's important—pierces through our gloves. I hear Luke's breath catch in his throat. Panic seems to leave his body, for just a second.

Good. Panic uses up too much air.

"We can take shifts digging," I suggest—but before I can even get the words fully out of my mouth, Luke's grabbed my hand with both of his, holding on to it like it's keeping him on solid ground.

"I know how to get us out of here," he says, with all the earnestness in his farm-boy-lookin' face. "But you have to trust me. And you have to let me do it."

I quirk an eyebrow at him. "Do what?"

He takes a deep breath, steadying himself. He swallows loudly. And then he says:

"Embrace the darkness."

It's not that I'm afraid of the dark. It's really not.

It's more that I'm afraid of what I might become if I spend too long in it.

But the fear and unfamiliarity of the darkness and what it could make me is something I'm getting used to. Not right away (as Reyé can obviously tell by my rapid breathing and the way I've potentially accidentally broken one or two of his fingers in my death grip). But slowly. Surely. I'm getting there.

And I know how to get us out of this. I have to.

Because that's what Jedi do.

Now, yes, there is another version of this where I had my lightsaber on my hip this whole time (which is also what Jedi should do, I'm learning very quickly), thus rendering the darkness, the snow, and probably the fork-nosed ice worm moot very quickly. So handy, my laser sword. So useful.

So sealed up in the decontamination unit where they've taken everything I was wearing before landing on Hoth to make sure I wasn't carrying any off-world pathogens that could harm the local wildlife.

Frankly right now I'm thinking maybe that wouldn't have been such a bad thing after all.

Still. No lightsaber.

But that doesn't leave me weaponless.

I tug Reyé down to the cold snowy floor of the tunnel with me and cross my legs. Still holding his hands, I close my eyes. I hear him let out another irritated sigh.

And then, through the Force, I feel him close his eyes, too.

I think about home. I think about Tatooine and those cruel, kind suns. I think of their light, reflected in Ghomrassen, Guermessa, and Chenini. I watch as every grain of sand in the desert absorbs the quiet light from those moons—and takes and takes until the moons dim and dim and then . . . there's nothing.

Tatooine is dark. Empty. Quiet.

But not entirely. In an instant, every grain of sand lights up—burning with the fire of both Tatoos. I watch as all the blazing sand lifts off the ground and floats into the sky, lighting the world back up again.

Setting it on fire. Burning it all down.

And then I hear Reyé gasp, and I'm back with my butt in the snow on Hoth. But now our clasped gloved hands are very, very warm.

Slowly, I open my eyes. And then I have to blink once, twice. It's so . . . *bright.*

Just to the left of us, like sun breaking through the clouds on Reyé's beautiful home planet, I can see it. I can *sense* it. The spot where the ice is thinnest, where the cave-in is most vulnerable to our soft human hands. Where, if we work together, for a little while, we'll be able to break through and find our way back to the light.

"I know where we can dig to free ourselves," I say, and I know I sound as wacky as Reyé thinks I am, but I'm right, and I don't care anymore what he thinks of me. I know I can save us. I *know* I'm right.

I look down at our faintly glowing hands and then back up at Reyé. I wouldn't say he looks happy; I don't think the guy has looked happy a day in his life. There's still some doubt in his eyes. But I will say—if I'm going easy on myself—that he looks *impressed*.

I flash the same big grin I gave him the first time I saw him. "See? Jedi aren't all bad."

He huffs, but I can see a little bit of humor in his eyes. "Solving the same problem you caused is supposed to make me like you?"

"*You* could have caused the problem, too, I'll remind you." He lets my hands go, and the glow fades slowly. But in the quickest flash, he's on his feet and offering me his hand again. "It's okay. I'll work on you. I have a feeling we're going to be on Hoth for a long, long time."

Reyé laughs—actually *laughs*—as he hauls me to my feet, the dark in his eyes gleaming. "Gods, I hope not."

And when we start to dig, it isn't long before the light breaks through, just like I saw in my mind's eye. The Force has never steered me wrong.

I know it never will.

MASTERS

TESSA GRATTON

DEEP IN COLD, black space, a half-built battle station waits. A superweapon. A Death Star.

A trap.

It blots out the stars, but twinkles with dangerous lights of its own. Because it is not yet complete, the Death Star Mark 2 looks like a great galactic beast has taken several bites out of it, leaving ragged edges. In orbit around the lush Forest Moon of Endor, the Death Star revolves slowly. Though it may look like a partnership between moon and star, there is a base on Endor that creates a massive deflector shield to keep the Death Star in place. The power required is slowly breaking up the little green moon—but that is an expected casualty. The Death Star is meant to destroy everything it touches.

At the north pole of the Death Star is a tower. One hundred stories tall, it is intimidating and elegant. Its master likes elegant things. He was born on a planet of elegance and raised himself to power on a planet of luxury. Of course his residence on his battle station would be a symbol of his tastes. But it is also a symbol of his domination over his ancient enemies, the Jedi. For centuries their temple on Coruscant was a beacon of hope and light, and they ruled from a gilded spire.

All their hope and light is gone now, eclipsed by the power of the master of the Death Star.

He has had many names. Some given. Some earned. Some taken.

Son. Sheev. Apprentice. Senator. Palpatine. Sith Lord. Sidious. Emperor.

But the one he likes the most is Master.

It was the first name of power he took for himself. A secret name, an invocation of the dark side. Spoken by his first devotee and by every apprentice since. Said with fear and awe, by those who have earned the right.

The weak call him Emperor. It is only those nearly as strong as him in the dark side who know his best name.

And one day soon young Skywalker will get on his knees and say it, too.

He has foreseen it.

At the top of the tower on the Death Star is his most brutal throne room. It is new, and he has never been here until now. But he looks forward to spending much time here, once he's crushed the last vestiges of the so-called Rebellion. The throne sits before a massive round window, and from it he can see all the galaxy. His galaxy. At his fingertips in the arms of the throne are control panels that connect him to the entire Death Star, from which he can command any person on any planet or ship across the span of the Galactic Empire.

Right now he does not use the technology to listen or speak. He does not let the workings of the million troopers and builders crawling around the battle station distract him. No, Emperor Palpatine leans back on his throne and looks out of the great window with his eyes and his feelings. The stars blur as the Force rises up in and around him. It is lightning under his skin. A network of crackling, furious energy in every direction. He feels everything around him: urgency, anger, fear, exactly what he seeks.

The Force draws his senses outward, onward.

He knows what is to come. He has sensed it. He has moved pieces here and there, arranged star systems to suit his plans. The last time he felt this anticipation was some twenty years ago, at the birth of his empire, when everything turned around the creation of his greatest asset: Darth Vader.

Vader has always been conflicted. Palpatine has always been able to use that conflict to his advantage, whispering, promising, manipulating Vader into those moments of singular clarity that make him so powerful in the dark side of the Force.

But no longer. This always happens with apprentices. Palpatine should know; he's had several. He once was one himself and recalls perfectly the moment he understood that he was better than his master, stronger and more powerful, and killed him. Palpatine will not allow any apprentice of his to reach that same realization—or think they have.

On his throne, he smiles. It is a cracked-lip, yellow-toothed smile. He is ugly. A gift from the dark side to make him more frightening, more awful before his time. He is on the outside what he is inside, and nobody who sees him could forget it. *Look at me. Fear me.*

It has been so long, so very, very long since anyone looked at him with anything but fear.

(He remembers. Determined eyes, golden with life, not yellowed by darkness. Grand Master Yoda. The green glow of Yoda's lightsaber against the bleeding red of his own.)

"I hear a new apprentice you have, Emperor. Or should I call you Darth Sidious?"

"Master Yoda, you survived."

"Surprised?"

"Your arrogance blinds you, Master Yoda. Now you will experience the full power of the dark side."

The Force lightning blazes to life in Sidious's veins, reaching hungrily for the old Jedi. Caught, Yoda is flung back, hitting the wall of the Office of the Chancellor hard.

"I have waited a long time for this moment, my little green friend," Sidious says as he stalks closer. Yoda does not move, except for the harsh rattle of his breath. Sidious laughs to see it. "At last the Jedi are no more."

Yoda pushes himself up and glares. "Not if anything to say about it I have!" He leaps up and with a pulse of the Force sends Sidious flying back into the opposite wall.

"At an end your rule is. And not short enough it was." With that, Yoda puts his feet in a battle-ready stance.

Sidious gets to his own feet. He has no need to duel this already defeated Jedi. He turns to go, but Yoda jumps in front of him and pushes back his cloak to reveal his lightsaber.

"If so powerful you are," Yoda taunts, "why leave?"

"You will not stop me," Sidious says. His rage fuels him, drawing sparks of the dark side closer and closer. "Darth Vader will become more powerful than either of us."

Yoda's ridiculously little lightsaber flares to life, brilliant green. "Faith in your new apprentice misplaced may be. As is your faith in the dark side of the Force."

In reply Darth Sidious merely ignites his own

lightsaber. The angry red fills him with eager cruelty, and he laughs. There is no need for faith in the dark side. The greater power of the dark side is simply a fact.

He attacks with another harsh laugh. Yoda flips up and around, parrying the attack and spinning with his own. The little Jedi Master is fast and bouncy, his movements making him difficult to pin down—but Darth Sidious meets him blow for blow. He cannot be defeated.

Their battle takes them to the half circles of the Chancellor's podium, sparks flying as their lightsabers clash. Using the Force, Sidious moves the lever that causes the podium to rise.

The ceiling spirals back, opening like a great eye, and beneath their feet the podium moves. It rises up and up like the Galactic Empire itself, into the Senate Chamber, a vast cave lined with over a thousand repulsorpods stacked in coiling petals. It is empty, silent, a theater without an audience for this show-down between Darth Sidious and one of the last Jedi Masters.

The two continue their battle, furiously, green and red lightsabers flashing together and apart. Darth Sidious laughs and laughs, his cruel cackle echoing against Yoda's grunts of effort. Sidious is enjoying himself. Crushing this old Jedi will taste sharp and sweet. But they are well matched. It is a rough fight. Exactly what Sidious craves.

A hard blow has him leaping away from the podium. He pulls on the Force to carry him across the cavernous Senate Chamber to land in one of the half-circle repulsorpods. Gleefully, he uses the Force to rip a different pod away from its berth and fling it at Yoda. He takes another and flings it, too. And another.

Yoda dodges, leaping away, but Sidious chases him, destroying pod after pod, like pulling scales one by one off the massive body of a krayt dragon. The old

Jedi tires and turns, and Sidious has him! He flings a repulsorpod, but Yoda catches it with the Force, both little green hands extended. Sidious laughs again, heady with the fury of the dark side. Suddenly the pod spins, and Yoda yanks it out of Sidious's control. The Jedi drives it directly at Sidious!

He has to leap out of its way, and the pod crashes into the one upon which he'd been standing with an explosion of sparks and fire. The thin smoke billows, and Sidious turns, leaps again, hunting for the Jedi Master. Where could the Jedi have hidden? Surely he did not slink away already in defeat!

Suddenly Yoda is there, hopping too fast to track, and Darth Sidious flings Force lightning at him. But Master Yoda catches it.

They face each other, cold blue lightning tying them together. Blue is reflected all around them, especially in the Jedi's determined, desperate golden eyes. Darth Sidious is tiring. He grins his worst grin and prepares a final assault with all the power of the dark side.

As if he sensed it, Yoda shoves back with a final burst of strength. Their power clashes, violently blowing them apart.

Darth Sidious catches himself on the rail of a repulsorpod, gasping for breath. He can barely breathe, energy surging through him as he pulls himself up. He turns to look for Master Yoda, laughing again.

All he sees is the Jedi's ugly brown cloak drifting down like discarded trash.

(The clone soldiers come, and they do not find a body.)

Now on the throne high in the spire of his isolation tower on the Death Star Mark 2, the Sith Lord, the Emperor, thinks about that old Jedi Master. Their unfinished duel.

It does not haunt him—he has no regrets that might cause a haunting. He won. So obviously he won. Grand Master Yoda slunk away to hide. Sidious rose to the apex of the galaxy. Everyone calls him Emperor now. Everyone fears him. Merely look at any corner of his galaxy and see evidence that he won.

But all the same, he'd like to end Master Yoda himself.

Not with his own two hands, of course. But with the shock of a red saber.

Collect Yoda's little lightsaber once the green creature is dead and set it with the others, with all his trophies in the Imperial Palace. It will look like a toy beside the rest. Useless, silly. There will be no one left called Master but himself.

He has looked. Set the Inquisitorius program to seek Yoda's hiding place. Made certain the hunter probes know his name and specs. Once or twice the Emperor considered various arcane Sith rituals that might instigate some kind of echo or thread of the

Force to lead him to Yoda's location. But he never performed them. Why bother? Why waste his own power on a mere irritation? Wherever Yoda is, his power is so diminished he can be no threat to the Empire.

But sometimes, when Palpatine sinks into the Force, drinking it up like the endless source of power it is, his feelings drift along distant threads of anger. Sparks of hate. And in a far-flung place he senses a fleeting moment of familiarity. It never amounts to anything if he bothers locating it. And over the years he has spent with the dark side, his feelings diffusing throughout and sucking up power, the very easy touch of Yoda's name has become meditative.

I defeated you. I chased you away and took everything that was yours. The things you stood for are ashes now. You remain, and as long as you do, I keep winning.

But the rest of the time, Palpatine prefers to see Yoda again, just long enough to watch him die.

He sits on his throne and stares out the massive viewport. He has sent the fleet away. Below the battle station hangs Endor, milky clouds just in his field of vision. Within a few short weeks, the jaws of this trap will snap closed around the Rebel Alliance. His apprentice will break a final time, and Vader's son will take his place. There will be no rebirth of the Jedi.

The Emperor smiles. And then he laughs. He hopes, after all, that Yoda lives. That old Grand Master Yoda will know when these final remnants of the Republic are crushed. That he will sense it, feel the pain of it. Yes. *Yes.*

(Vader is coming, approaching the space dock to speak with his master about the search for his son, and he feels the Emperor's satisfaction pouring through the dark side.)

Far, far away on a mossy planet thick with brackish waters and tangled swamp trees, a Jedi Master is dying.

He does not think about his old rival at all.

Instead he lets himself spread out through his

feelings and into the Living Force. He knows this planet inside and out. It seems to breathe with him, sometimes, especially now that his breathing is staggered and thick. All around him life thrives. Vines tremble, and wide-faced fuchsia blooms turn toward his little house nestled in the roots of a gnarltree. Swamp slugs and spotted rodents go about their own tasks; bogwings and dragonsnakes scream happily in the thick air. Tiny insects buzz, wild and jagged, others caught in the webs of grimspiders who are eager to feed their thousands of babies. The Force pulses through them all, light and clear. Yoda sighs. The Force sighs, too.

This place has been a refuge for him. Brimming with the light side of the Force. A crushing amount of life. That is what he thinks about in his last moments. The Living Force. The way it diffuses throughout the galaxy. Wondrous even in the colder places, like that cave. It is part of the Force, too. Everything turns in cycles. That is the way of life. And this boy in front of him. So eager. So rash. So bright. Just like those who have come before him.

Yoda is tired.

He stands at his hearth, leaning slightly against the rough wattle wall. The fire is warm; he is colder than he's used to—both because of the Force and because of this always-hot planet that has been his home for decades. Nothing seems to warm his bones now. Luke Skywalker is speaking to him, denying Yoda's gentle teasing.

Yoda turns. His joints ache. "When nine hundred years old you reach, look as good, you will not. Hmm?" At the young man's expression, Yoda giggles. He has missed children. Though this one is too old for what he is learning. Still just as reckless as a child. Yoda huffs softly and makes his way very slowly to his bed. "Soon I will rest. Yes, forever sleep." It sounds restful. He will be with the Force. He hefts himself onto the low bed. "Earned it, I have."

"Master Yoda, you can't die." Despite the growing

concern in Luke's tone, it is amusing to see the tall young man crouched in Yoda's hut like an Elphronan firestork in a stolen nest.

Yoda sighs. "Strong I am with the Force, but not that strong." Carefully he lowers himself onto the thin pillow. "Twilight is upon me, and soon the night must fall." Oh, he's grown poetic in his dying moments, and he wishes one of his old friends were here to laugh at him. Luke Skywalker is too serious. Too young to understand. But the youth takes the blanket and raises it up to Yoda's shoulders. Good of him. The boy is good. He must stay good. Yoda says, "That is the way of things. The way of the Force."

He closes his eyes. He is so very tired.

"But I need your help. I've come back to complete my training." The boy is urgent. So urgent. The emotion wafts off him. Urgency, need, expectation . . . of loss. Veering too close to fear.

Keeping his eyes closed, Yoda says, "No more training do you require. Already know you that which you need." He sighs very softly. It is true, but Yoda does not know if young Skywalker will understand.

But hope surges from Luke. "Then I'm a Jedi?"

Yoda's eyes fly open with a spark of life, and he laughs. It becomes a dry cough. "Ohhh, not yet." He pauses to gather his words and give time for Luke to even out his disappointment. Yoda says, "One thing remains: Vader. You must confront Vader." And he looks Luke right in the eye. "Then, only then, a Jedi will you be. And confront him you will."

Yoda cannot help thinking now of the last Skywalker. Anakin is there in Luke's eyes. Yoda forces himself not to look away from it. From how everything turns around again. Rainy season to dry to rainy once more. Master . . . apprentice . . . master. He feels himself drifting into the cold ache of his old bones. His eyelids are heavy.

Luke says, hesitating, "Master Yoda . . . is Darth Vader my father?"

It is a fair question, but Yoda does not want to

answer. He rolls over, turning away from the young Jedi. "Mmm, rest I need. Yes . . . rest."

"Yoda, I must know." There is a gaping need in Luke; Yoda feels it. A longing for connection, for family. And behind it, that fear.

Yoda remains turned away. His breath creaks in his lungs, and he closes his eyes before he admits the truth. "Your father he is."

Silence stretches between them, though the Force is anything but silent as the young man roils internally.

"Told you, did he?" Yoda asks. It is interesting. Dangerous. If Darth Vader wishes a connection with his son, it can only lead to greater power of the dark side. But this is not for Yoda to puzzle out. He has no time.

"Yes," Luke says.

"Unexpected this is. And unfortunate."

A surge of upset comes from Luke. "Unfortunate that I know the truth?"

"No." Yoda grunts as he turns back around.

"Unfortunate that you rushed to face him. That incomplete was your training." He must say this. It hurts, but he leans up to get closer to Luke. "Not ready for this burden were you."

"I'm sorry."

"Remember . . ." Yoda gasps as he tries to push the words out. No one is ever ready for these kinds of confrontations. With destiny. With a Sith. With a father. "A Jedi's strength flows from the Force." It is too difficult, and Yoda lays himself back down. "But beware. Anger . . . fear . . . aggression, the dark side are they. Once you start down the dark path, forever"—he gasps again—"will it dominate your destiny. Luke . . . Luke . . . do not . . ." Yoda can barely keep his eyes open. This is important. Luke must understand. Learn from Yoda's mistakes! He underestimated Palpatine long ago. Thought he could face the Sith Lord and win. Look . . . look where it got him. He says to Luke, "Do not underestimate the powers of the Emperor, or suffer your father's fate you will! Luke . . . when gone I am, the last of the Jedi will you be."

Yoda pauses to breathe. His ear is folded uncomfortably against the pillow, but he cannot move.

Luke Skywalker says nothing, but through the Force Yoda feels the young Jedi's awe. And his fear. And a resurgence of that need to connect—to his father. Family. Yoda would tell him. There is more family. Not only Vader. Must not rely on Vader.

"Luke, the Force runs strong in your family. Pass on what you have learned. Luke . . ." No time. The Force is everywhere. All around him. It feels so warm. And Yoda is so tired. But he must—he says, "There is another . . . Sky . . . walker."

With that final word, Yoda stops. The Force inside him and around him is vivid, loud. The entire planet breathes with him. Once more. Then not at all.

He is not tired anymore. He is the Force. With it. Always has been. Always . . . will be.

His corporeal body vanishes.

The Force is wondrous. Master Yoda is no longer a piece of it. He *is* it. But he remembers himself as he was taught. He remembers who he is, who he has been. He remembers who he will be. Though he does not breathe, he remembers how to laugh.

(But something out there in the galaxy also remembers him and is calling his name. Right now.)

The Emperor feels it. Maybe because he was thinking about the old Jedi again. His thoughts and feelings already turned in that inevitable direction.

Grand Master Yoda. Dead. As if he's always been able to feel the ancient green Jedi and suddenly his presence is gone.

No—it's the opposite. It is as if Yoda has not existed at all to the Emperor, and suddenly he is all around. Everywhere in the Force.

The Emperor hisses and pulls on his anger, always

ready to stoke those flames for the dark side. He is filled with it, the glorious power, lightning under his skin. The Emperor laughs. He laughs and laughs.

Yoda is *dead*.

"Oh, Yoda," he says to himself, teeth bared in a hideous smile. His laugh echoes throughout the throne room, from observation window to sitting area to docking bay doors, across the bridge that narrows over the giant pit. Blue glow pushes up from that chasm, from the thermal reactor at the heart of the Death Star, a cold contrast to the sickly red light of the isolation tower.

Even the Imperial Guard stationed to either side of the docking bay doors shift in discomfort at the eerie triumph of the Emperor's laugh.

Then—

Then the Emperor feels a thrill in the Force. And—

Impossible!

Yoda stands before him, hazy and surrounded by a glow as if lit from within.

It *is* impossible. And yet . . .

Yoda. Hunched and ancient, in his old Jedi robes with that gnarled walking stick.

The Emperor does not know if this is real, but he bites out a final laugh. "You are dead."

The ghost inclines his head.

"But come to watch my final glory? I hoped you would see it." The Emperor spins slowly on his throne to face the observation window. He raises a hand to sweep across the expanse of stars. "Not long from now I will crush the Rebel Alliance. And take the newest Skywalker as I took his father!" The Emperor cackles again.

Behind him, the strange vision of Yoda speaks in that same rough little voice. "Win, you cannot."

This makes the Emperor nearly shriek with laughter. "But, Master Yoda, I *already have.*"

He turns back on his throne, eager to see Yoda's frown.

But the specter is gone.

(Later, as the Rebel Alliance begins its attack on the Endor moon base and the fleet is ready to spring the Emperor's trap, he sits on his throne again, eager and waiting. He senses the approach of Darth Vader, and with Vader—his son. The Imperial Guard sends an alert to the throne that Vader's ship has docked, and the doors hiss open. The Emperor turns, alight with triumph. "Welcome, young Skywalker," he says. "I've been expecting you.")

THROUGH THE TURBULENCE

ROSEANNE A. BROWN

REY COULD NOT BELIEVE that of all the millions of billions of people in the galaxy, she was stuck spending the afternoon with Poe Dameron.

She knew Poe wasn't a bad person. Rey trusted General Organa, Finn, and BB-8 with her life. If they cared about him as much as they did, there was no way he could be malicious or cruel. It was just that he was . . . a lot to deal with sometimes.

Like right now.

"If you're looking for new tension cables, the X-89A series is way better than the T-45B," said Poe, leaning against the wooden pole of a market stall with his arms crossed. They were on the planet Thorat IX, a tiny rock of a world deep in the Outer Rim, trying to buy supplies for the *Millennium Falcon*. The Resistance was still reeling from the Battle of Crait, and Thorat IX had been chosen as a safe stop due to the lack of First Order presence on the planet.

Still, even knowing they were temporarily safe from the faction's hold, Rey's nerves were on edge. Was that black mass in the distance a tent or a First Order ship? Was that flash of white a droid or a stormtrooper? This errand was nerve-racking enough without Poe's constant interjections.

Rey took a deep breath, mentally reciting the meditation General Organa had advised her to practice to keep her temper from getting the best of her. "The *Falcon* is an older model, which makes the T-45B the safer choice. It doesn't have the engine power to run on the X-89A," she said, gesturing at the pile of blue cables laid out on the table before her.

Poe shook his head. "I've flown rust buckets that'd make the *Falcon* look like it came straight out of the shop. They all handled the X-89As fine." He nodded at the pile of red cables sitting next to the blue ones. "If you don't want to repeat this same purchase on the next planet we go to, get those instead."

Rey gritted her teeth and looked down at BB-8 for assistance, but the orange-and-white droid only let out a beep that made it clear he was staying out of this one. Much like everyone else in the Resistance, the astromech was tired of Rey and Poe's constant bickering. That was the very reason General Organa had ordered them on this routine supply run, claiming that if she had to sit through another one of their thinly veiled arguments, she'd hand them over to the First Order herself.

Instead of rising to Poe's bait, Rey turned to the shopkeeper—a stout orange-furred being with a monocle over one eye—and said, "Four T-45B cables for *my* ship, please." She barely hid her smirk at the muscle that twitched in Poe's jaw at the reminder that even though he might have more pilot experience than her, she still had final say on all things *Millennium Falcon* related. At least when Chewie wasn't around.

She wondered if Master Luke would scold her for her rather un-Jedi-like pettiness. But thinking about her former mentor was a mistake, because every thought of him ultimately led her back to that moment when she felt him become one with the Force. Rey's chest constricted as a thick haze flooded her senses, like the world was somehow both too quiet and too loud at the same time. The T-45B cables clutched in her shaking hands, she quickly walked deeper into the market, Poe and BB-8 on her heels. Maybe if she walked fast enough, she could outrun the grief.

"We need to keep moving. General Organa was very clear that we need to be back at the ship within the next three hours or else." Rey glanced up at the sky, which was a familiar bright blue with slightly less familiar bright yellow clouds rolling across the horizon. Several duo ships flew past, an outdated model of plane that required two pilots working together to fly. They'd been discontinued in most places in the galaxy due to how difficult they were to maneuver, but clearly the population of Thorat IX had not gotten the memo.

Right now the sky was simply pretty, but in three hours that same air would be filled with sickly pink fog composed of a poison strong enough to corrode the metal off even a Star Destroyer. The fog came and went, but if they were still there when it returned, the *Millennium Falcon*—and by extension the Resistance— would be stranded on Thorat IX for weeks before it dissipated. Then they'd be sitting ducks for the First Order, which Rey would not allow on her watch.

"I'm well aware of that. I attend the morning briefings, too," said Poe, with that charming smile that seemed to work on everyone but Rey.

Luckily, all they had left to buy were rations. Then Rey and Poe would be done with this errand, and with each other, for at least the rest of the day. They stopped in front of a food stall filled with pyramids of produce, most of which Rey had never seen before. She reached for one of the few she recognized, a round blue tuber that wasn't the tastiest but was the cheapest. However, Poe made a sound of dissent.

"If you buy those, everyone on the ship is going to be keeled over in the refresher," said the pilot. "Forget the First Order, diarrhea will be what takes the Resistance out in the end."

"I used to eat paeyu fruit back on Jakku. It's not that bad," Rey argued, her desire to not snap back forgotten. "Maybe it's not as fancy as what you grew up with, but if you haven't noticed, we're on the run. We don't have a lot of options here, and General Organa told me to purchase whatever I felt suited our needs best."

That muscle in Poe's jaw twitched again. "So you and the general just talk all the time now, huh?"

What was with that tone? Maybe Rey didn't have war hero parents like Poe did, but was it so hard to believe that General Organa might trust her with things she didn't trust others with? "Yeah, we do."

Well, maybe not *all* the time, but Poe didn't need to know that. General Organa had been pivotal in helping Rey manage her grief over Master Luke, but there were still some things Rey didn't dare tell the older woman about.

Rey and Poe stared each other down. A small, petty part of Rey wanted to use the Force to upend the entire pyramid of paeyu fruit over the pilot's smug head. But she wouldn't, of course. That would be a *very* un-Jedi-like thing to do (even if it would be hilarious . . .). But, more important, she couldn't.

Rey was having a hard time tapping into the Force these days. Her connection to it felt muffled; it was still there, but every time she tried to reach it, her thoughts would get too jumbled and unfocused for her to connect. It had been that way ever since Master Luke died. General Organa already had so many problems on her plate that Rey didn't want to add another one, and no one else on the *Millennium Falcon* was well-versed enough in the Force to help her.

But Rey would let a happabore eat her before she let Poe see she was struggling.

Poe shattered the tense silence first. "Beebee-Ate, break the tie for us, buddy. Should we buy Rey's nasty nightmare fruit, or something that is actually edible? . . . Beebee-Ate?"

They both looked down at the space between them.

But it was empty.

A shrill beep tore through the air, and Rey looked up just in time to see BB-8 in the clutches of a trio of purple-scaled creatures she didn't recognize, who were racing away with the astromech as fast as their limbs could carry them.

"Hey! Get your claws off my droid!" bellowed Poe. Hearts in their throats, he and Rey charged after the kidnappers but quickly lost their trail in the labyrinth of bodies and stalls. Both of them doubled over from exhaustion, Rey saw her own dread reflected in Poe's eyes as the realization hit them:

BB-8 was gone.

Rey and Poe scoured the market for nearly an hour before they found someone who could explain what had happened. According to a cloak seller covered in dozens of furs, the beings who had taken BB-8 were known as the Qoogai. They lived in the tunnel system deep beneath the surface of Thorat IX and rarely interacted with outsiders. The cloak seller led them to the tunnel's entrance, a smooth hole carved into the cliff face that bordered one side of the market. Judging from how little light emanated from the tunnel's depths, the path went very, very deep.

The next thing they did was contact General Organa.

"That's droids for you. Always getting into some mess or other," the general said when they explained the incident, and Rey could practically hear the smile in the Resistance leader's voice through the communicator. However, her tone was serious when she continued, "Go look for him, but know there's only two hours or so until the poison fog returns. If you can't find him by then, we'll have to leave without him. I know how much he means to you, but we can't risk the fate of the Resistance over a single droid."

With that solemn warning ringing in their ears, Rey and Poe plunged into the tunnels in search of their friend.

It took less than a minute of walking for Rey to decide she did not like that place. At all.

The tunnels were both dark and damp, lit every few meters by eerie green crystals that cast a pallid glow over her and Poe's skin. It was like walking down the throat of some giant glowing beast, as if any second the walls could close in and swallow them within that world forever.

If only Luke's old lightsaber hadn't shattered in two. Another light source would've been wonderful right—no. No more thoughts of Master Luke. *Not here, not now.*

"See anything?" Rey called out to Poe.

The pilot shook his head. "There's not enough dirt on these rocks for tracks. There aren't even scuff marks, so they must have carried him in. He could be anywhere down here." Poe glanced up at the crystal-studded ceiling. "We've gotta be, what, fifty, one hundred meters below the surface right now? I've got no clue how much time we've lost."

Fear curdled tight in Rey's stomach, but she pushed it aside. She tried once again to reach into the Force to see if she could get any sense of life or even movement within the rocks—nothing. But that didn't matter.

They were going to find BB-8 before the Resistance left Thorat IX without them.

They had to.

But with each step and minute that passed, the droid felt farther and farther away. Rey crossed her arms over her chest as horrible images of what the Qoogai might've done with BB-8 flashed across her mind.

"Why do you think they took him in the first place?" she whispered. There was no need to talk quietly since there was no one else there, but she was too nervous to speak louder.

"Parts, most likely. BB-8 is one of the newer models on the market. Pull him apart and you could make a fortune on his core pieces alone."

Rey shuddered. "How can you talk about that so coldly?"

"I'm not being cold, I'm being realistic," Poe shot back. "We both know they didn't nab him just so they could have him over for biscuits and tea."

"All I know is if Beebee-Ate were my droid and he'd been kidnapped, I wouldn't be making jokes about it!"

"Oh, so now you're trying to steal my droid on top of my mentor!"

Poe's eyes went wide, as if he hadn't meant to say what he'd just said. Rey stared at him. He had to be referring to General Organa.

"What's that supposed to mean?" she demanded, but the pilot was already jogging toward a new tunnel.

"It's nothing. Come on, we haven't checked this super creepy dimly lit shaft yet."

Rey ran after him. "Don't change the subject! What do you mean I'm stealing your mentor?"

"I said, it's no—*GAH!*"

The words were barely out of Poe's mouth when the ground gave way beneath him. All Rey saw were streaky blurs of green light as she and Poe tumbled head over heels through the tunnel floor, landing with a bone-jarring thump in a spacious cavern that looked like the inside of a rainbow.

Instead of the sickly green crystals that populated the rest of the tunnel system, this cave was filled with orbs of every color and material imaginable. Metallic spheres hung suspended by wires from the ceiling, while other circular objects poked out of shallowly dug holes in the rock. Still more rolled freely across the ground in the wake of Rey and Poe's ungraceful landing. There were orbs of brightly colored glass, orbs of soldered-together metals, orbs of some pulsing biomass, and much, much more.

And there, in the middle of the chaos, in a round cage on top of a rocky pedestal, was BB-8.

"Buddy!" cried Poe, and his voice was so raw with relief that Rey regretted implying for even a second that he didn't care enough about the droid.

When her head finally stopped spinning, Rey sat up, unstrapped her staff, and cautiously poked one of the biomass orbs. "I guess this explains why the Qoogai wanted him so badly," she mused. The creatures clearly had a fondness for round things.

Poe was halfway to BB-8's cage when a trio of

beings stepped in front of him. The Qoogai were a tall race, easily rivaling Wookiees in height, but with scaly purple skin instead of fur, and six arms instead of two. All three hissed something at Poe in a lyrical language that neither he nor Rey understood. He blinked in surprise before flashing them his tried-and-true Dameron smile.

"Um, we come in peace?"

Less than five minutes later, Rey and Poe were both in a metal cage to match BB-8's. While they waited for their captors to decide their fates, the droid filled them in on what had happened since his abduction. Apparently he'd tried beeping for help when the Qoogai leader had first grabbed him, but Rey and Poe had been too focused on their argument at the fruit stand to notice. Rey saw her own guilt mirrored on Poe's face. How could they call themselves Resistance fighters when they'd been so deep in their own petty argument that they hadn't even heard their friend calling for help?

"I'm so sorry, buddy. It won't happen ever again," Poe swore, and Rey nodded along. BB-8 let out a series of offended beeps that made it clear it better not.

"Beebee, how much time do we have left until the poison fog returns?" asked Rey. There was a low hum, and then a single virtual number one projected out of the astromech's body. Rey's stomach plummeted to her feet. One hour. They'd wasted too much time!

While the Qoogai fawned over a giant ball of dirt that one of their friends had rolled into the cave, Poe tested the bars of their cage. "Okay, clearly the fastest way out of this is a little lightsaber action."

Rey grimaced. "Luke's lightsaber is still broken. General Organa thinks it can be fixed, but I haven't figured out how yet," she said. It stung to admit there was something she could not do, especially to someone like Poe, who did almost everything perfectly.

Well, not counting his mutiny on the *Raddus*. That definitely hadn't gone so well.

The pilot sighed. "Okay, new plan: you use the Force to trick our gracious hosts into letting all three of us go, and then we hightail it out of here before they come to their senses."

Rey hugged her knees close to her chest, suddenly wishing the rocks had buried her in the cave-in so she wouldn't have to have this conversation. "I can't," she whispered.

"Rey, I've seen you use the Force to lift boulders the size of Wookiees. What do you mean you can't mind-trick a handful of Qoogai?"

"Because I can't do anything anymore!" The words exploded out of Rey before she could stop herself. "My mind is a cluttered, jumbled mess, and I can't get through it to reach the Force!"

It was the first time Rey had told anyone of her problem. She'd managed to keep it hidden most of the time, acting like her usual self whenever Finn, General

Organa, or anyone else in the Resistance was around. But in the rare moments when she was alone, whenever she'd sit and try to clear her mind like Master Luke had taught her, all she'd see was him fading away into starlight and nothing. She'd be thrown back into the chaos of the battle in Snoke's throne room and the hurt she'd felt when Kylo Ren had betrayed her just like everyone had said he would. All those thoughts would crowd her mind until they were dense as a forest, leaving no path through which she could get to the Force.

Rey expected Poe to be disappointed. She expected him to tell her how much trouble the Resistance was in now that their resident Force user couldn't do any of the things that made her useful.

She didn't expect Poe's face to soften with understanding.

"How long has this been going on?" he asked gently.

"Ever since Master Luke . . . Ever since he . . . Since Crait." Rey hugged her knees more tightly, making herself small like she'd used to do back on those lonely nights on Jakku. "I haven't even told General Organa yet. She's going to be so disappointed." After all, what kind of Jedi couldn't even use the Force?

Several emotions warred over Poe's face before he scooted closer and put a comforting hand on Rey's shoulder. "Hey, if the general can forgive me for literally trying to steal control of her army, I'm pretty sure she'll forgive you for not being able to lift some rocks."

Rey let out a dry laugh. "That's easy for you to say. You've known the general your whole life. You're practically family. But me? I'm just an orphan who stumbled onto the Resistance. I bet if Luke's lightsaber hadn't called to me on Takodana, the Resistance wouldn't even know my name."

Poe's face twisted in anger. "You really think we're that shallow? Not just me and General Organa, but Finn and everyone else who believes in you, you think that little of them, too?"

From his cage, BB-8 let out several beeps of agreement. Rey shifted away from Poe.

"You wouldn't understand."

"On the contrary, you seem to be forgetting that our esteemed general literally stunned me with a blaster not that long ago. I understand how it feels to disappoint her. The Resistance doesn't demand perfection from its members, Rey. If you're willing to stand with us, you belong with us."

Tears welled up in Rey's eyes. "Even if I can't use the Force ever again?"

"Being connected to the Force isn't the most important thing about you or what makes you matter to us. And besides, something tells me this block you're having isn't permanent," replied Poe. "You know how sometimes when you're flying, everything will be perfectly clear as far as the eye can see, then out of nowhere you'll hit a cloud of turbulence? Right now, you're in the middle of the cloud and it feels like it'll never end. But when you hit those rough patches, you can't just shut down your engine and hope for the best. The only way out is through. And when you get to the other side, things will be clearer than they've ever been."

Poe's eyes took on the far-off look of someone sinking deep into a memory. "What you're feeling now, I've been there. Honestly, some days I'm still there. After everything with Holdo . . . some days are harder than others. But know that I'm right there with you, finding my way through the turbulence. If I can do it, you can, too."

It was as if a rock had been lifted from inside Rey's chest. Poe's words alone didn't make all her guilt about the past and nerves about the future go away, but it felt easier to deal with them knowing they weren't forever.

"Thank you," she said, and Poe gave her a small smile.

"Hey, you're one of us now. The Resistance, we take care of our own." He paused, pulling a face. "Even if you are still wrong about paeyu fruit."

Rey let out a real laugh for the first time in a long time, which was quickly interrupted by a series of distressed trills from BB-8. The Qoogai had finished their deliberations and were picking up the droid's cage to carry it deeper into the tunnels. Rey and Poe had to act fast, before they were separated from their friend again.

Poe looked around wildly until his eyes lit up with an idea. "Paeyu . . . that's it! You still have that nasty fruit?"

Rey did in fact still have the nasty fruit. She handed the paeyu to Poe, who said, "When I give the signal, you grab Beebee-Ate and run."

"What about you?" asked Rey, but Poe had already turned his attention to the Qoogai. He waved the paeyu fruit in front of him as if it was the most sacred treasure in the galaxy. "Hey, if you guys like round things, then do I have the fruit for you!"

The Qoogai immediately swarmed Rey and Poe's cage. One of them reached a spindly purple arm through the bars to grab the paeyu, but Poe snatched the fruit back toward his chest.

"No way. If you want to see this up close, you have to open the door."

Rey didn't think anyone would fall for that, but clearly she'd underestimated just how much the Qoogai loved spheres. They scrambled to open the cage door, and the second the bars sprang free, Poe launched himself at their captors. The Qoogai had taken his blaster from him, but Poe was more proficient in a hand-to-hand skirmish than Rey would've expected. He climbed onto the back of one Qoogai before elbowing the second in the gut and kicking the chest of the third. Rey hurried out of their cage and over to BB-8's while Poe grappled with the trio.

Rey picked up one of the crystal orbs and used it to bash the lock on the cage until the droid was free. She gave him a quick pat on the head before scanning the cave for an exit. There! Up ahead, there was a tunnel that would likely lead them back to the surface. She and BB-8 might even make it to the *Falcon* before the poison fog returned.

However, Poe was still busy with the Qoogai. Rey could run with BB-8 or go back and help Poe fight, but there wasn't time for both. Panic washed over her at the thought of Poe being stranded on this planet at the mercy of the Qoogai. The Resistance had already lost too many good people—good friends. They couldn't lose him, too.

Ignoring her instinct to run to safety, she turned back to where Poe and the Qoogai fought, BB-8 close behind her.

Rey took a deep breath, tapping into that place within her where the Force lived. She imagined her mind full of turbulence, like Poe had described. This time, instead of trying to fight it, Rey let the cloud envelop her completely. It was scary, but just like Poe had said, it wasn't endless. She imagined herself taking one small step through the cloud, and then another, until she was reaching a hand into the clarity she had been missing for so long.

Just like that, Rey knew what she had to do.

"You are going to let my friend go and escort us back to the surface as fast as possible," she said to the Qoogai leader.

The words of the mind trick fell easily off Rey's tongue, lending her voice the kind of authority she'd never had growing up. The Qoogai leader's eyes went slack, and they yelled something to their companions in their lyrical language. All three immediately pulled away from Poe, who looked a bit scuffed up but lacked any major injuries. Rey helped him to his feet, BB-8 supporting his other side, as the Qoogai leader twitched one of their six arms in the universal gesture for *Follow me*.

Despite the bruise purpling on his lip, Poe smiled at Rey as they followed the Qoogai out of the orb shrine and toward freedom. "Looks like someone found their way through the turbulence."

Rey smiled back. "Luckily, I had a pretty great pilot to guide me. Now, let's get out of this place while we still can."

They were too late.

When Rey, Poe, and BB-8 reached the surface of Thorat IX, the markets, the vendors, and the tiny community that had been bustling on the bright purple sand just a few hours earlier had vanished. So, too, had the *Millennium Falcon*. Billowing clouds of pink smog rolled across the horizon, heading straight for the tiny marketplace. A few brave ships flew into it—but none flew out. The Qoogai had scurried back into their underground sanctuary, safe from the fog's effects.

Terror clawed up Rey's spine. They'd taken too

long. Now they'd be stranded until the First Order found them or the poison fog got them, whichever came first.

But Poe was ever the optimist, and he refused to consider a situation lost until all options had been well and truly exhausted. He pointed toward an abandoned duo ship not far from the fruit seller's stall.

"The poison fog hasn't set in completely. If we leave now, we should be able to reach the top of the atmosphere before the toxins start eating the ship."

It wasn't the best plan Rey had ever heard, but she didn't have a better one.

Unlike most ships, where there was a clear primary pilot and secondary one, each flier in the duo ship controlled one of the double engines. Rey and Poe had to be in perfect sync if they didn't want to crash and burn.

Poe took the right engine, Rey took the left one, and BB-8 nervously rolled into the astromech socket.

"All right, Beebee-Ate, give us some juice!" called

Poe, and one jump start by the astromech droid later, the duo ship was ricocheting into the sky.

The difference in Rey and Poe's flying styles was immediately apparent. Poe's movements were all loose grace and speed, while Rey was a fan of more controlled if slower maneuvers. The ship twitched and jerked, the engines fighting each other in an attempt to reconcile the conflicting flight patterns. The unmistakable groan of collapsing metal filled the cockpit as the poison fog began to eat at their ship's frame.

BB-8 let out a series of shrill beeps, and Poe grit his teeth.

"I know you're scared, but there's no need for that kind of language," he scolded. He looked at Rey, terror in his eyes, though his voice was steady when he said, "We can do this. Together."

Rey nodded. They both turned to their respective controls with new determination. The ship shuddered again before losing altitude so fast that BB-8 banged against the cockpit wall with a heavy thud.

They were going down.

Down.

Down . . .

Until they were going up.

The duo ship shot into the sky with a rise in altitude almost as sharp as the dip had been. Rey incorporated a little more of Poe's speed into her approach while Poe added a little more of Rey's caution into his. The engines finally hummed in harmony now that they could work in that sweet spot between each pilot's style. The duo ship flew up through Thorat IX's atmosphere with surprising control, weaving in and out of the fog plumes with expert skill.

But though they were fast, the poison fog was faster. Rey imagined it like giant formless hands determined to grab ahold of them and never let go. The ship shuddered again, and little warning lights flashed across the dashboard that they were starting to lose their critical systems.

Rey and Poe pushed the duo ship to the very

edge of its power. But this was no X-wing fighter or *Millennium Falcon*. Even with the two pilots, the duo could move only so fast.

But then, up ahead through the gloom was the most beautiful sight Rey had ever seen: the outline of the *Millennium Falcon* moving quickly out of range of the poison fog. They'd made it!

Rey immediately keyed into the special comm channel only Resistance members could access.

"Open up! It's us! It's us!" she cried before the *Falcon* could start shooting.

And in the first stroke of luck all day, the ship's cargo door opened, revealing Rose and Finn waving wildly in their direction with wide grins on their faces. It took a bit of careful maneuvering, but soon Rey, Poe, and BB-8 were all safely in the belly of the *Falcon*. The last of the Resistance shot into hyperspace, Thorat IX nothing more than a memory in the rearview.

Rey and Poe had done it.

And more important, they had done it together.

"That had to be the galaxy's worst errand run," said Finn, and Rey was so relieved to see him that she wasn't even mad at the teasing. She hugged him hard, and he hugged her back. Curious as ever, Rose wanted to know everything about the planet, the species there, and the poison fog.

Just as comforting as being with her friends again was the knowledge that when Rey'd needed to most, she'd been able to find her way back to the Force. The battle ahead would be a difficult one, and there would never be a day when she didn't mourn Master Luke and everyone else they'd lost. But part of being a Jedi meant moving forward even when the past tried to hold you back. The path wasn't always easy, but it was Rey's, and she'd fight her way through it every time for the sake of those she loved.

Rey and Poe exchanged glances, a new understanding between them in light of their shared experience. Maybe the two would never see eye to eye on everything, but they were no doubt on the same side. That mattered way more than their differences ever would.

Then Poe leaned against the wall, the vision of easy confidence, as if he hadn't been wrestling a trio of Qoogai and losing not too long before.

"You see, our intrepid adventure today began, would you believe it, with Rey being wrong about cables and fruit."

Rey let out a long-suffering sigh.

The more things changed . . .

ABOUT THE AUTHORS

JENNIFER BRODY (writing as Vera Strange) is the award-winning author of the Disney Chills series, the Continuum Trilogy, and the Stoker-nominated graphic novel *Spectre Deep 6*. She is also a graduate of Harvard University and a creative writing instructor. She began her career working in Hollywood on many films, including *The Lord of the Rings* and *The Golden Compass*. You can find her on Twitter @JenniferBrody, and Instagram and Facebook @JenniferBrodyWriter.

ROSEANNE A. BROWN is an immigrant from the West African nation of Ghana and a graduate of the University of Maryland, where she completed the Jimenez-Porter Writers' House program. Her debut novel, *A Song of Wraiths and Ruin*, was an instant *New York Times* best seller, was an Indie Bestseller, and received six starred reviews. She has worked with HarperCollins, Marvel, and Scholastic, among other publishers. You can visit her online at roseanneabrown.com or on Instagram or Twitter @rosiesrambles.

SARWAT CHADDA is a *New York Times* best-selling author who swapped his passion for old-school tabletop gaming for a career in writing back in 2009. Since then he's written novels, comic books, and TV series, including *Devil's Kiss*, *The Legend Of Hanuman* for Disney+ Hotstar, and the best-selling *City of the Plague God*. His writing embraces his heritage, combining East and West, with a particular passion for epic legends, vicious monsters, glorious heroes, and despicable villains. Having spent years traveling, he now lives in London, but has a rucksack and notebook on standby. Find him on Twitter as @sarwatchadda.

DELILAH S. DAWSON is the author of the *New York Times* best seller *Star Wars: Phasma* and *Star Wars Galaxy's Edge: Black Spire, Minecraft Mob Squad: Never Say Nether, Mine, Camp Scare, The Violence*, the Tales of Pell series (with Kevin Hearne), the Hit series, the Blud series, and the Shadow series (written as Lila Bowen), as well as the creator-owned comics *Ladycastle, Sparrowhawk*, and *Star Pig*, plus comics in the worlds of *Firefly, Star Wars, The X-Files, Adventure Time, Rick & Morty, Marvel Action: Spider-Man, Disney Descendants, Labyrinth*, and more. Find her online at delilahsdawson.com.

TESSA GRATTON is genderfluid and hangry. She is the author of *The Queens of Innis Lear* and *Lady Hotspur*, as well as several YA series and short stories that have been translated into twenty-two languages. Her most recent YA novels are *Strange Grace* and *Night Shine*, as well as the forthcoming *Chaos and Flame*. Though she has traveled all over the world, she currently lives alongside the Kansas prairie with her wife. Visit her at tessagratton.com.

MICHAEL KOGGE is a best-selling author and screenwriter from Los Angeles. His original work includes the graphic novel *Empire of the Wolf*, a werewolf epic set in ancient Rome. He's also written books for many high-profile properties such as *Star Wars*, *Harry Potter*, *Fantastic Beasts*, *Game of Thrones*, and *Batman v Superman*. His adaptation of *Star Wars: The Rise of Skywalker* won the 2021 Scribe Award for best young adult novel. You can find him on Twitter @michaelkogge or on the web at michaelkogge.com.

SAM MAGGS is a best-selling writer of books, comics, and video games, including Marvel's *The Unstoppable Wasp: Built on Hope*, *Star Wars Adventures* for IDW, and the upcoming *Knights of the Old Republic* remake. A Canadian in Los Angeles, she misses Coffee Crisp and bagged milk.

MICHAEL MORECI is a screenwriter, best-selling comics author, and novelist. His debut feature film, *Revealer* (which he wrote and executive produced), was released on Shudder in 2022. In the comics space, Michael is the cocreator of the sword-and-sorcery series *Barbaric*, the existential space opera *Wasted Space*, the gothic horror series *The Plot*, the werewolf drama *Curse*, and many more original titles. He's also written for numerous legendary characters and properties, including *Star Wars*, *Stranger Things*, and *Batman*. He currently lives outside Chicago with his wife and kids.

ALEX SEGURA is an acclaimed, award-winning writer of novels, short stories, and comics. His work includes the comic book noir *Secret Identity*, *Star Wars: Poe Dameron: Free Fall*, *The Black Ghost*, *The Archies*, the Pete Fernandez Miami Mystery series, and more. A Miami native, he lives in New York with his wife and kids.

KAREN STRONG is the author of middle grade novels *Just South of Home* and *Eden's Everdark*. Her short fiction has appeared in *From a Certain Point of View: The Empire Strikes Back* and *A Phoenix First Must Burn*. Born and raised in rural Georgia, she grew up cosplaying Princess Leia. Visit her at karen-strong.com.

ABOUT THE ILLUSTRATOR

JAKE BARTOK is a freelance comic book artist and fantasy illustrator. Known for his high-concept fantasy works, he has been illustrating comic books; collaborating with authors, musicians, and game companies; and sharing independent projects online since 2016. He fell in love with a galaxy far, far away in 1999 at the midnight premiere of *The Phantom Menace*, and it has continued to inspire his work ever since. Jake lives in Australia with his wife and their dog, Samwise.

ABOUT THE EDITOR

JENNIFER HEDDLE is an executive editor at Disney Publishing Worldwide. She edits *Star Wars* books for children, teens, and adults, working out of Lucasfilm's headquarters in San Francisco. She lives in the East Bay with her husband and their rescue kitty.